BOOKS BY JAN MORAN

Summer Beach Series

Seabreeze Inn

Seabreeze Summer

Seabreeze Sunset

Seabreeze Christmas

Seabreeze Wedding

Seabreeze Book Club

Seabreeze Shores

Seabreeze Reunion

Seabreeze Honeymoon

Seabreeze Gala

Seabreeze Library

Seabreeze Harvest

Seabreeze Garden

Coral Cottage Series

Coral Cottage

Coral Cafe

Coral Holiday

Coral Weddings

Coral Celebration

Coral Memories

PRAISE FOR USA TODAY AND WALL STREET JOURNAL BESTSELLING AUTHOR JAN MORAN

***Seabreeze Inn* and *Coral Cottage* series**

"A wonderful story… Will make you feel like the sea breeze is streaming through your hair." – Laura Bradbury, Bestselling Author

"A novel that gives fans of romantic sagas a compelling voice to follow." – *Booklist*

"An entertaining beach read with multi-generational context and humor." – *InD'Tale* Magazine

"Wonderful characters and a sweet story." – Kellie Coates Gilbert, Bestselling Author

"A fun read that grabs you at the start." – Tina Sloan, Author and Award-Winning Actress

"Jan Moran is the queen of the epic romance." —Rebecca Forster, *USA Today* Bestselling Author

"The women are intelligent and strong. At the core is a strong, close-knit family." — Betty's Reviews

The Chocolatier

"A delicious novel, makes you long for chocolate." – *Ciao Tutti*

"Smoothly written…full of intrigue, love, secrets, and romance." – *Lekker Lezen*

The Winemakers

"Readers will devour this page-turner as the mystery and passions spin out." – *Library Journal*

"As she did in *Scent of Triumph*, Moran weaves knowledge of wine and winemaking into this intense family drama." – *Booklist*

The Perfumer: Scent of Triumph

"Heartbreaking, evocative, and inspiring, this book is a powerful journey." – Allison Pataki, *NYT* Bestselling Author of *The Accidental Empress*

"A sweeping saga of one woman's journey through World War II and her unwillingness to give up even when faced with the toughest challenges." — Anita Abriel, Author of *The Light After the War*

"A captivating tale of love, determination and reinvention." — Karen Marin, Givenchy Paris

JAN MORAN

SEABREEZE
Harvest

A Summer Beach Novel, Book Twelve

SEABREEZE HARVEST

SUMMER BEACH
BOOK 12

JAN MORAN

Library of Congress Cataloging-in-Publication Data
Moran, Jan.
/ by Jan Moran

ISBN 978-1-64778-338-9 (epub)
ISBN 978-1-64778-339-6 (paperback)
ISBN 978-1-64778-340-2 (hardcover)
ISBN 978-1-64778-343-3 (large print)
ISBN 978-1-64778-342-6 (audiobook)
ISBN 978-1-64778-341-9 (large print)

Published by Sunny Palms Press. Cover design by Okay Creations. Cover images copyright Deposit Photos.

Sunny Palms Press
991 Lomas Santa Fe Dr. Suite C-113
Solana Beach, CA, USA 92075
www.sunnypalmspress.com
www.JanMoran.com

May every day be a feast at the table of life with close friends and family.

1

———

wave of excitement swept through Ivy when her brother unveiled the rendering for their new project at the kitchen counter. Forrest had included a sign that read, "The Amelia Erickson Library and Art Museum."

"I never imagined the project would look like that," she said, easing onto a stool in her paint-splattered jeans and sneakers. Earlier today, she'd been finishing a seascape painting for a client in her studio. "It's truly stunning."

Forrest gestured toward the plans. "Your former owner had tremendous foresight. Very impressive for a small beach town."

"But is it too much now?" Ivy drew in her lower lip, trying to imagine how the new structure would look in the village of Summer Beach.

Her husband tapped the image. "That's why the city needed this rendering," Bennett replied. "Residents will have the opportunity to voice concerns if they have any. It's better to get their buy-in and approval before the final plans are approved. That's the way Boz manages the process for the city."

Ivy sensed some concern on his part. After all, Bennett was the mayor of Summer Beach. "Is there a chance this won't be approved?"

"There's always that risk, but in this case, I think it's minimal," he replied.

Ivy folded back the sleeves of her shirt and studied the drawing on the countertop. This image of what the new library and art museum would look like was based on the architectural plans the inn's former owner had commissioned decades ago. Several months ago, Lea Martin, Amelia's long-lost great-niece from Germany, had generously funded this cultural center in Amelia's memory.

"It's beautiful and quite grand," she said. "I love it, but do you think it will look out of place now?"

Forrest shifted on his stool. "The white stucco and red-tiled roof of the Spanish Colonial Revival and Mediterranean styles will complement the inn. When the Ericksons built your place, Las Brisas del Mar, they were probably envisioning the entire town in that style."

"Much of it is," she said. From the beach bungalows that dotted the Summer Beach shoreline to the estates on the ridgetop, many were built like that.

Yet her brother wasn't answering her question. Before they fully committed to the updated plans, she had to be sure this project was in the best interest of their beach town.

Ivy considered the sketch. "We all know the inn stands apart from everything around it. I want the library and museum to fit its surroundings."

Bennett looked at her with a trace of amusement. "You think it's too pretentious now?"

"Seeing it drawn like this looks different from the blueprints. I worry that this is too fancy for Summer Beach kids in shorts and sandals. It might be intimidating."

"Or inspiring," Bennett added.

Ivy could understand his point. "But where's the fun and whimsy that would draw people inside? Like Libby's creative bookmobile does."

Bennett and Forrest stared at her, not quite grasping what she meant.

She tried again. "Let's share this sketch with the community and listen to feedback. I don't want Bennett to take the heat for a project I'm leading. I'm the mayor's wife now, and people can be critical."

Bennett put his arms around her and kissed her forehead. "Trust the process. We'll have a council meeting open to the public for questions and suggestions, and we'll ask the paper to print it to reach even more residents."

Ivy thought of her neighbor, who could be cranky about change. "Then there's Darla to think about. She has a clear view of that land."

"Tell her it will raise her property value," Forrest said, grinning.

Initially, Ivy's neighbor had been receptive toward the project, but she'd complained about the construction noise at the inn, and now, the inconvenience of the library project, despite the eventual convenience of having a library within walking distance.

Still thinking about Amelia's vision and her habit of hiding items in the house, Ivy gazed at the drawing. An odd feeling flitted through her, as if she were missing a crucial piece.

The accomplished art collector had suffered from Alzheimer's disease, but before that, when the Second World War spread across Europe, Amelia had rescued important art and artifacts from Germany with the help of her father, who had overseen a museum there. She'd also helped resettle artists and innovators who'd managed to flee Europe.

Ivy and her sister had discovered art items and more that Amelia had hidden in the house for preservation.

That was a story that should be preserved.

How could she honor Amelia's personal accomplishments, besides realizing her vision for the library and museum? This rendering was perfect.

Maybe too perfect.

That's it, she thought, before blurting out, "This lacks Amelia's appreciation of creativity."

Frowning, Forrest leaned in. "What do you mean by that?"

"It's a museum, so it needs art that has an authentic vision." She snapped her fingers. Suddenly she knew. "Like Gaudí in Barcelona."

"Who?" Forrest asked.

"A celebrated architect who lived in Spain. Antoni Gaudí created whimsical designs that furthered the Catalan Modernism and Art Nouveau trends in the first part of the twentieth century. Have you ever seen photos of the Parc Güell? The mosaics are magnificent, as if sprouted from nature. So creative and joyful, a pure explosion of exuberant colors."

While her reference sparked a small light in Bennett's eyes, her nephew's stare was blank.

"Look it up," she said, growing excited. "Gaudí's work has always captured my imagination. Maybe we can hire a contemporary artist to create fanciful accents. I know there are some in Southern California. I just don't know who they are."

Yet, that is.

Still, the two men didn't share her vision. Bennett and Forrest might be trying to understand her artist's soul, but they weren't there yet.

"I'll show you some examples later," she added.

Forrest nodded to appease her. "In the meantime, we need to survey the land to determine the topography and confirm easements and property lines."

Ivy recalled the day they'd christened the site for the library and art museum. "When you look at the topography, will you also look at what's below the surface? I'm thinking about what my shovel hit when we had the kick-off celebration. It seemed like old concrete. Or maybe it was metal."

"The survey will identify any issues that might affect construction," Forrest said. "There's a natural rise in elevation on that land. What you hit might have been an old drainage pipe or a large rock. We find all sorts of things when we begin excavation for construction. Finding old relics, fossils, or graves will slow down the process."

"How will we know what's down there?" Ivy asked.

"You won't, not until we begin the excavation."

She wondered if they should wait that long to find something that might hamper the project schedule.

Just then, the kitchen door burst open, and Shelly

stepped inside, holding a toddler on her hip. Her wavy, sun-bleached chestnut hair was windblown, and little blond-haired Daisy clutched a picture book. They both wore sundresses with sandals.

Ivy greeted her sister and niece with hugs. "Is that a new story from the bookmobile?"

Shelly smoothed her daughter's fine hair. "We were playing on the beach when Libby parked her bookmobile nearby. Daisy squeals every time she sees that magical vehicle, so we had to visit."

Ivy sent a pointed look at Bennett and Forrest, but the proof was lost on them.

Shelly nodded toward the plans. "How is the new project going?"

"I didn't realize how many details there'd be, but it's coming together," Ivy replied. "Thanks to our amazingly talented brother."

Daisy's eyes widened at the rendering. She cooed with delight and pointed at it.

Bennett laughed. "There's your first resident approval."

"That will be an incredible building," Shelly said.

Bennett leaned in. "Too much?"

Shelly made a face. "I think too much is just about right. Don't let people scare you. Although Summer Beach could use something quirky, like Laguna Beach's artistic influences."

"That's exactly what I thought," Ivy said.

Bennett grinned. "Okay, I know that look on your face, sweetheart."

"Well, it is an art museum." She tapped the rendering as ideas whirred through her mind. She would figure it out.

Shelly gestured toward the plans. "This was Amelia's

vision for the town. So I'm all in. Do you know if something else was built there before?"

"Not that we know of," Ivy replied. "Forrest thinks I hit an old drainage pipe."

He nodded in agreement. "Something like that. The Gutierrez family bought the property to build a family compound, but their situation changed before they could develop it."

"Maybe you should check out that old pipe," Shelly said, raising her brow pointedly at her brother.

Forrest shook his head. "We'll address that after we break ground. No sense having men and equipment out there at this point. That would be a waste of time and money."

Bennett nodded along with him. "That makes sense. Besides, people often dump debris on vacant land."

"But we all know what Amelia was like," Ivy said. "What if she buried something there?"

"Sweetheart," Bennett said, covering her hand with his. "Let your brother handle the construction. He knows his business best, just as you know yours."

So surprised was Ivy at his words that she was momentarily speechless, searching for the right reply. She met her sister's questioning gaze, reading her mind as clearly as if she'd spoken.

But before she could think of a comment or retort, Bennett cleared his throat and turned to Shelly, swiftly changing the subject as if he were in a city council meeting, not in the kitchen with family. "Are you and Mitch ready for the wine harvest party tomorrow?"

"We wouldn't miss it," Shelly replied slowly, tearing her gaze from her sister. "How about you two?"

Ivy was a little perturbed at her husband, but she also knew he and Forrest were only doing what they thought was right. And maybe they were, but the thought of something buried on the property still bothered her. Even if it was just an old piece of concrete.

Because what if it wasn't?

Ivy shifted her attention to the conversation about the weekend's plans. Fortunately, the high season was over, so Poppy and Sunny had agreed to look after the inn while they were away for the weekend.

Emilie and Tristan Boivin owned a winery and vineyard in the nearby mountains. The French couple was celebrating the grape harvest season with an event they called the crush. She and Bennett had been looking forward to it.

"We're going to have such fun this weekend," Shelly said, her eyes sparkling. "Ivy, will I see you at the book club meeting later tonight? It's at Ginger's cottage this time."

Ginger Delavie was a local legend who lived in a beach house everyone called the Coral Cottage. Ivy was friends with her granddaughters.

"I can give you a ride." When Shelly arched an eyebrow, Ivy knew exactly what her sister was thinking. And she was all in on it. She hadn't come this far with transforming a rambling old beach house into an inn without taking a few outlandish risks.

A plan was already forming in her mind as Forrest and Bennett excused themselves to return to work.

As soon as they left the kitchen, she confirmed her suspicion with Shelly. They agreed to include their niece, Poppy.

After the sun set, Ivy changed into a pair of dark jeans and a black knit turtleneck. She quickly loaded shovels into the trunk of her 1957 cherry-red Chevy convertible, wincing as the metal scraped. She closed the trunk, trying to be quiet and feeling a little guilty, as if preparing for a heist.

"Hey, sweetheart." Bennett appeared on the balcony above her, silhouetted against the light spilling from their apartment above the garage. "Are you headed to your book club meeting?"

She smiled up at him, smoothing over her awkwardness. "Almost. I'm waiting for Poppy."

Grinning, he held up a book. "Don't forget this." He jogged down the steps, holding the novel the book club members had been reading. "Looks like you've barely cracked the spine."

"I listened to the audiobook on my errands and walks." She had been so busy with the end of the season activities at the inn, she had barely kept up with the book club.

She took the book from him, feeling the weight of her scheme settle between them. "Thanks, honey."

Bennett kissed her forehead. "Have fun. Call me if the wine flows too freely. Wouldn't want Chief Clarkson to pull you over."

"Don't worry. I'm the designated driver." She kissed him.

Poppy hurried toward them with a book tucked under her arm. Fortunately, she remembered hers.

Bennett opened the door for Ivy, and she slid behind the wheel to start the car. The engine turned over with its familiar rumble. She pulled away from the inn, watching her husband wave in her rearview mirror.

Poppy glanced back in the mirror. "Did he suspect anything?"

"No, and he still doesn't understand why this is so important."

Guilt pricked at her, but not enough to turn back. Bennett had agreed with her brother and taken his side over hers. Even when she brought it up again this afternoon, he'd told her to let Forrest check out the site and do his job.

He'd also seemed irritated, which wasn't like him, and she wondered if the call he'd taken earlier had something to do with that. *Just city business*, he'd said.

Their weekend getaway couldn't come at a better time. Maybe she wasn't the only one with slightly frayed emotional edges.

Poppy turned to her. "This is exciting, but are you sure we're doing the right thing, Aunt Ivy?"

"If Amelia buried something there, I want to know before bulldozers and backhoes turn the site into a construction zone and damage whatever might be underneath by accident. It would be too easy to forget and lose an important piece of history or Amelia's story."

This history mattered to her, as she felt a connection with the woman whose passion for art she shared. But it was more than that. During the war, Amelia Erickson had risked her life to give shelter to people and transport historical and cultural artifacts to safety.

What more might she have accomplished had Alzheimer's not robbed her of her memory?

Only uncovered during the recent renovation, the plans for a library and art museum had revealed one of Amelia's intentions for Summer Beach. Ivy was determined to see the project through now.

They drove to Shelly's bungalow, where she emerged

wearing a similar pair of dark jeans and a black hoodie like she'd dressed for a mission. Mitch stood in the doorway, holding Daisy on his hip. His spiky, sun-bleached hair shone under the porchlight.

"Back by ten, babe," Shelly said, sliding into the backseat.

Instead of turning toward their friend's cottage down the beach, Ivy drove the short distance to the vacant lot slated for the future library and art museum.

Streetlights flickered on, casting pools of amber light across empty sidewalks. The lot sat across from a row of boutiques, now closed.

No traffic. Minimal lighting. Perfect conditions for covert excavation.

Ivy parked on a side street across from the lot, and they hurried to get the shovels.

"This still feels a little wrong," Poppy said, pulling a flashlight from a toolbox.

Ivy handed her a shovel. "It's our project. We have every right to be here."

Poppy hefted the tool. "Then why are we creeping around like we're about to rob it?"

"Because men like to mansplain," Shelly said, picking up another shovel. "Sometimes it's easier to do a job yourself than try to convince another person of its importance."

As she shut the trunk, she caught a glimpse of what looked like a young, slender man on the street in a dark faded hoodie and jeans. She didn't recognize him, and he hurried away.

She waited until he was gone before crossing the street.

The lot smelled of dry grass with a whiff of eucalyptus

from the trees lining the street. Somewhere nearby, a dog barked, then fell silent.

Poppy switched on the flashlight. The beam swept across the vacant lot, illuminating a sign that read, "Future Home of The Amelia Erickson Library and Art Museum."

Beyond that lay the raised area near a volunteer palm tree where Ivy had hit something hard.

The trio walked across the lot to the spot she remembered.

"Here goes." The earth resisted as Ivy's shovel bit in.

"Keep the light low," Shelly whispered to Poppy. "We don't want it visible from the street."

"Then how are we supposed to see?" Poppy angled the beam downward, creating a small circle of illumination.

"Carefully." Ivy scooped out the soil she'd loosened during their ceremonial groundbreaking. She and Shelly worked their shovels against the rest of the hard-packed earth.

"Let's try another section," Ivy said, repositioning her shovel.

After a few minutes, Ivy rested her arms on top of the shovel, catching her breath. "This is ridiculous to be out here like this," she said, realizing the folly of the situation. "We have every right to investigate this property in the daylight, regardless of what Forrest and Bennett think."

"Then why are we sneaking around like crooks?" Poppy asked.

"Because we want to find the treasure first," Shelly said, her eyes glimmering in the light.

Ivy dug her shovel into the ground again. "And if we wait for the excavation crew and they find something, the whole project stops. Do you know what construction loan interest runs per day?"

"More than I want to think about," Poppy replied. "Want to switch off with me?"

Just then, Ivy's shovel struck something solid. The vibration traveled up the handle and into her wrists. "Found it."

Shelly knelt immediately, brushing away loose soil so they could all see. "It's not a pipe. Feel that; it's flat."

Ivy crouched beside her, tracing the top of whatever lay beneath them. The surface felt smooth, deliberately finished.

"I think it's metal." Ivy pressed harder, trying to gauge the size. The object extended beyond the small pit they'd created.

Poppy shifted the flashlight, leaning closer. "What do you think it is?"

A deep voice boomed behind them. "Good evening, ladies."

Poppy dropped her flashlight, spinning a wild beam across their faces.

Ivy's heart pounded. Caught in a blinding beam of light, she froze.

Chief Clark Clarkson stood behind them holding a brighter flashlight. His patrol car sat at the curb with the lights off.

"Clark." Ivy straightened too quickly and nearly lost her balance. Her shovel clattered against the buried object. She held up her hand, shielding her eyes against the brightness. "We were just…" She wasn't sure how to explain this.

"Digging up this property in the dark. I can see that. Mind telling me why?"

Shelly stood, wiping her palms on her jeans. "Ivy hit

something with her shovel. Our brother thinks it's an old drainage line under here, but we don't."

Clark nodded slowly, mentally assembling the puzzle before him. "And given Amelia Erickson's track record, you wanted to check before the construction crew tears through here, am I right?"

"That's about right," Ivy said.

Clark lowered the flashlight and inclined his head. "Smart thinking but terrible execution. Why do it at night?"

Poppy recovered her flashlight. "We didn't want to attract attention."

"You attracted the attention of a very concerned neighbor who called in suspicious activity." Clark's gaze drifted toward the residential street, where curtains glowed in several windows. "Three people with shovels and a flashlight after dark raises questions."

Shelly's eyes widened. "Did someone think we were out here burying a body? That would have been spooky. Imagine, a real murder mystery right here in Summer Beach."

"Darla," Ivy muttered, throwing a look at Shelly to be quiet.

Clark's mouth twitched, but he didn't confirm it. "Whoever it was had a right to call. You want to dig? Do it in daylight. You're the mayor's wife, and you control this property. No one's going to stop you from investigating the land at a reasonable hour."

"We acted on impulse," Ivy said, trying to ignore the guilty twinges in her chest.

"And you just happened to have shovels in your car." Clark crouched beside their excavation.

He ran a beam of light along the exposed edge of the buried object. After a moment, he straightened. "Could be anything. Could be nothing. But if it turns out to be significant, you'll want documentation with photographs and proper handling. You've been in similar situations at the inn, so you know what to do."

"We wouldn't be here except for Ben—" Ivy cut herself off, feeling a little embarrassed. Clark had a reasonable point, and she sounded like a teenager shifting blame. Not her finest moment.

He met Ivy's gaze. "That's between you two. Just continue whatever you're doing in daylight. And give me a call before you start, so I know not to respond to any more concerned citizen reports."

Ivy nodded, understanding his point of view. "I wasn't thinking about that."

Shelly put a hand on her hip. "Go easy on Ives. She was only thinking about our mansplaining brother and his partner in crime."

Clark motioned for them to follow him. "Like I said, if Amelia Erickson buried something here, it's waited this long. It can wait until daylight."

Hastily, Shelly and Ivy shoved dirt back into the hole, tamped it down, and scraped dry leaves over it all.

Clark walked them back to Ivy's car, waiting as they placed the shovels in the trunk. Ivy started the engine, breaking the quiet night.

"Drive safely," Clark said. "And ladies? Next time you plan a covert operation, consider that Darla watches this area like it's her personal domain. She'll see you, even if you dress in dark clothes like a bunch of bandits."

Ivy managed a weak smile. "So noted."

Clark stood beside his patrol car, waiting until they left.

As Ivy pulled away, Poppy broke the silence. "What now?"

Ivy glanced at Shelly in the rearview mirror. "We come back after the weekend."

Her sister leaned forward. "But we're so close. How about in the morning?"

"We have guests," Ivy said. "That means breakfast, the morning walk, and yoga classes."

"Don't forget the early check-in family," Poppy added. "We can't all disappear without explanation and leave Sunny in charge."

Ivy checked the time. "We might as well go to the book club now."

Shelly and Poppy muttered their agreement, so she turned toward Ginger's cottage, the Chevy's headlights cutting through the darkness. "Let's circle back next week on a slow day. Sunny can watch the inn when it's quiet."

"And if we don't find anything?" Poppy asked.

"Then Forrest and Bennett get to say, 'I told you so,' and we move on." Ivy pulled up outside the cottage, where laughter spilled from open windows. "But if there is something..."

Shelly opened her door. "Then we'll have found it first."

"Don't forget the books," Ivy said.

She wondered how they would manage the next few days thinking about what Amelia Erickson might have buried beneath the future library.

Would Clark mention this to Bennett? She might have to let her husband in on this operation after all. Their actions might have been foiled tonight, but soon enough they'd find out what had been buried there.

Tonight, the book club meeting was more about planning for the upcoming holiday season in Summer Beach than discussing the book they'd read, although they did that, too.

After the meeting, Ivy piled into the car with Shelly and Poppy. She would drop off Shelly before returning to the inn.

As they passed Java Beach, Shelly sat up and pointed. "Oh, my gosh, what happened? The outdoor chairs have been thrown all over the place. Ivy, pull over. I've got to call Mitch."

Poppy looked out. "And look at the building. We should call the chief, too. Maybe it's a robbery."

Ivy pulled to a stop, gaping at the side of the building. Far from graffiti or urban folk art, angry slashes of black spray paint were hastily rendered and deeply disturbing. Last year, Mitch hired a local artist to paint a charming vintage beach scene on the side of the building.

Mitch answered, and Shelly put him on speakerphone. "Mitch, something happened at Java Beach." Quickly, she told him what they saw.

Keys jangled in the background, and Mitch's voice was stern. "Call the police. Stay away, and don't go in there. I'll come to you in a few minutes."

"What about Daisy?"

"She's coming with me. We're already out the door, so get out of there."

Poppy had already dialed the police. When the dispatcher came on the phone, she gave them the address and told them what happened.

Her heart pounding, Ivy started the car, pulled across the street and parked farther away. She turned off the lights. Interrupting a robbery, if that's what it was, could be dangerous.

While they waited, Java Beach remained dark and silent, with no discernible movement inside.

Shelly rubbed her forehead. "Who would destroy such a beautiful painting?"

"Someone angry with an obvious grudge," Ivy said, watching the area for any movement. "Has Mitch mentioned anyone giving him trouble? Customers or former employees?"

Shelly shook her head. "Most people love Mitch."

In the rearview mirror, Ivy saw a police car pull up in front of Java Beach. Two young officers got out to walk around and inspect the property. Chief Clarkson arrived and joined them.

Ivy watched them circle the building, shaking their heads.

Mitch pulled up behind them in the Jeep, his lights off. With Daisy in his arms, he raced toward her. "Take her and stay here. I'll talk to Clark."

"It doesn't look like they found anything," Shelly said, taking Daisy, who watched the unusual activities with wide eyes. She ran her little hands over the red leather seats, cooing at the bright color.

Mitch gazed at the spray-painted destruction on the wall with dismay. Grim faced, he said, "I need to see if they gained entry."

Shelly pressed Daisy to her heart. "You're such a good girl. Stay quiet for me."

The toddler seemed to understand and looked around with curiosity, watching while her father spoke to the police officers. They went inside and emerged again shortly afterward.

Mitch gave them an all-clear signal with a wave.

Shelly let out a breath. "Oh, thank goodness it wasn't worse."

"Clark's a great guy but seeing him twice in one night on police business is a little much," Ivy said.

"I can't tell Mitch what we did earlier now," Shelly said, chewing her lip. "He won't be in the mood to understand." She blinked as Mitch strode to the car.

"Nothing was disturbed inside," he said, blowing out a breath. "The chief says it's probably random vandalism, but I'm not so sure. Tomorrow, they'll check to see if anyone saw anything. Jen and George have cameras on the hardware store, so maybe those recorded something. There's nothing we can do tonight, babe."

"I'm so relieved," Shelly said, smoothing her hand over Daisy's back. "Can we leave now?"

"I've got to finalize the report, but you can all go. I'll meet you at home. We have a big day tomorrow."

2

The next morning after breakfast was finished and early weekend guests had checked in, Ivy tidied the kitchen. The events of last night weighed on her mind. Her nocturnal dig paled in comparison to the vandalism at Java Beach.

Shelly appeared in the doorway, zipping her seafoam-green hoodie. "The yoga class is over, and all the guests are happy. Back to reality now."

Ivy emptied the dishwasher as she spoke. "Any news about Java Beach?"

"Mitch told me some of the patrons swore there was a gang of three dressed in dark clothes sneaking around the village last night."

Ivy froze. "You're kidding. You'd think they would've seen the red Chevy, too."

"You didn't park right by the lot. Even if they did see it, no one would suspect you. At least Clark knows who that trio was and that we wouldn't vandalize Java Beach."

Ivy's heart thumped. Should they be worried? "I hope he believes that. Maybe we should call Imani."

The retired attorney now ran the flower stand in the village, but she'd helped Ivy sort out several thorny legal issues. And now she was dating Clark.

Shelly pitched in to help put away the dishes as they talked. "Actually, I'm more concerned about Mitch."

"How is he taking it?"

"You'd think he'd be furious, but he says he understands where the person was coming from. I mean, he's still upset, but he's surprisingly chill about it. That's not normal, is it? Maybe he's depressed."

Shelly's husband had a tough upbringing. Long before she met him, he'd spent a year in prison. He'd been at the wrong place with the wrong friends and made a bad decision regarding a stolen car.

Ivy put up the last of the clean glasses. "We should tell Mitch those rumors are wrong."

"Please, let's wait until after the weekend," Shelly said, clasping her hands. "We've been looking forward to this event, and we all need it."

Slowly, Ivy nodded. "Agreed. But we will tell them. I don't want any of this to be misconstrued, especially if anyone recognized us."

Shelly threw her arms around Ivy. "That's a relief. As soon as I drop off Daisy at Darla's, and Mitch finishes food prep at Java Beach, we'll leave for the winery. We all need to breathe in the crisp mountain weather and have a change of pace. What time do you plan to leave?"

"Soon," Ivy replied. "Poppy and Sunny want me to look at a new autumn ad program before we leave. This is shaping up to be a good weekend, but I'm concerned about future reservations. They're slowly coming in, but I want to make sure they continue throughout the off-season."

"Sunny said she booked a nice reservation from a doctor."

"That's a good start. We should plan something new. Maybe a homemade gift fair the first week in December. The crafters in Summer Beach would have a chance to gain some customers, too."

"Let's work on some ideas." Shelly paused. "Back to this weekend. Hope you got a pedicure, and most of all, don't forget swimsuits for you and Bennett."

"Done and done." Ivy arranged the wine bottles and glasses on the counter for Sunny and Poppy. "I sure need a break after the renovation and the summer season came so close together."

Shelly grinned as she brought out a tin of crackers and added it to Ivy's advance setup for the evening tea and wine event. "I promise this grape harvest celebration will be an event like you've never seen before. Trust me; it will be a real blowout."

Ivy narrowed her eyes, wondering what Shelly was up to. "I know you too well. I'd rather trust Emilie and Tristan."

"You'll see," Shelly replied, quirking a grin. "Just be sure to bring your sense of humor. See you at the winery."

"Do you have everything?" Bennett asked as he put their overnight bags into the SUV. They'd also packed lightweight jackets in case the evenings were cool. They were acclimated to the warmer beach weather.

"Everything that matters," she said, handing him a beach bag with their swim gear, though they wore jeans and boots for their mountain trip. "At the top of that list is you, sweetheart."

Bennett smiled and kissed her cheek as he helped her into the vehicle. He wasn't acting like Clark had said anything to him about seeing her, Shelly, and Poppy last night. That information could wait until they returned. Still, she wondered about the vandalism at Java Beach.

"Do you know if the police discovered who defaced the beachside mural at Mitch's place?"

Bennett put on his sunglasses and shook his head. "I'm sure the police are working on it. Maybe they'll find an eyewitness."

"I heard some people were seen."

"Suspicious, sure, but we'll see." He reached for her hand. "Mitch is being philosophical about it. Some of the regular patrons have started a fund to repaint the mural. He says that's good news for the artist, who needs the work. In a funny way, I suppose it is."

Ivy slid on her sunglasses and let that conversation drop. She hoped Mitch wouldn't lose money and was glad the artist would benefit.

They chatted about their family and the upcoming holidays as they drove, leaving behind beaches and palm trees for mountains and pine trees. Ivy loved the change of foliage in the fall, and she took photos as Bennett drove to remember it.

She'd been thinking about a series of autumn paintings for a change from her usual seascapes. The black oak trees were turning yellow, and the sycamores were transforming with blushes of amber and blazes of red.

"It's beautiful up here," Bennett said, following the winding roads with practiced ease.

"I'd like to spend more time here in the fall and winter," Ivy said, resting her hand lightly on his shoulder.

He nodded as he drove. "It's a world apart from where we are, yet so close. We need this calm more often."

"Emilie and Tristan will probably see snow at their elevation later this year. I'd love a wintry weekend some-time." She paused, thinking about his reaction yesterday about the library and museum project. "Summer Beach is awfully busy during the summer, and I've been focused on the inn. Has anything happened lately?"

Bennett's hesitation was barely perceptible, but she sensed it.

He patted her knee. "No more than usual."

They spoke a little more, and Ivy managed to work Clark and Imani into the conversation. Bennett didn't seem to have spoken to Clark this morning, so she relaxed a little, then immediately felt a twinge of guilt for not sharing what she'd done last night.

She loved her husband, but in this case, she was deter-mined to follow her gut instinct, especially since he'd seemed out of sorts yesterday. She knew his job wasn't an easy one, even in Summer Beach. Residents had differing opinions. Sometimes Bennett compared his mayoral job to that of a referee.

She decided she was doing the right thing by sparing Bennett another conversation about her plan. He would know soon enough if they found anything.

After a couple of hours, they arrived at the intricate iron gates that stood open to Château Boivin.

Emilie and Tristan greeted them at the door to their

home with open arms. They were about the same age as Ivy and Bennett, and they had moved to Southern California from France to grow grapes and make wine years ago.

"*Mes amis*, welcome," Tristan said, his face wreathed with a smile. He was dressed casually in denim jeans and a jacket.

Emilie's dark hair framed her face in soft waves. She embraced Ivy and kissed her on both cheeks, speaking in a melodic tone laced with a soft French accent. "I'm so glad you could join us. We have a fabulous weekend planned for you."

"What's on the agenda?" Bennett asked as he brought their small bags from the car.

Emilie traded a secret glance with her husband before she said, "Wine, of course. Relaxation, fun, and friendship. We want you to share this wonderful celebration with us."

From their expressions, Ivy could tell they clearly had a surprise in store. Shelly seemed to know what it was, but she wasn't letting on.

"We're looking forward to spending time with you," Ivy said. "This is the first relaxing break we've had in months."

"Then you are long overdue," Emilie said.

Ivy gave her a hostess gift of gourmet items from the farmers market she had assembled for them, knowing how much they enjoyed delicacies. Strawberry preserves, olive oil, and a small loaf of pumpkin bread that she'd made. Hanging on the entryway door was the wreath Shelly made for them.

Emilie thanked her and tucked her arm into Ivy's. "Come, I'll show you to your room. After you've freshened up from your journey, I'll introduce you to our friends."

Over the years, their friends had added guest rooms onto the main house and built cottages on the property, which they rented to those wishing to escape hectic lives for the tranquility of life in the vineyard. Much as Ivy did, Emilie and Tristan hosted weekenders, weddings, honeymoon couples, and writers' retreats.

The last few years, Ivy welcomed the couple to the inn after their harvest, and Emilie and Tristan returned the favor.

"You've redecorated," Ivy said, gazing around the room that overlooked the vineyard. An art glass chandelier of vines and purple grapes glowed from the ceiling. "Where did you find this unusual piece?"

"From a local artist," Emilie replied, plumping a pillow on the bed. "She is a master glassblower in the old tradition from Italy. We fell in love with her work. I made the pillows to match."

Ivy and Bennett promised to join them for a welcome reception. "You mentioned a special surprise tonight. Is there anything we should prepare for?"

Emilie's eyes sparkled with mischief. "Just be yourselves. I promise it will be an unforgettable experience. But I will take your swimsuits with me now. We'll go to the hot tub later, and you might not want to come back here to change."

Clearly, her friend had a plan. Ivy was intrigued, so she gave Emilie their swimsuits.

After their hosts left them alone, Bennett turned to Ivy and took her hands.

"What do you think that's all about?" Ivy asked.

"We'll learn soon enough. Come with me, sweetheart." He led her to the balcony.

The vineyards stretched before them, and the sun slipped toward the mountains that separated this land from the sea. Vines laden with ripening fruit glowed in the waning rays, and fresh, earthy aromas filled the crisp air. Leaves rustled above, and Ivy glanced up to catch a glimpse of a hummingbird before it flitted away.

Bennett nuzzled her neck. "Let's take a breath and reconnect before we join the others. Just us for a moment, my love. Look at where we are."

Whether he meant the vineyard or where they'd arrived in life didn't matter. She lifted her face and touched her lips to his, enjoying their intimate connection. The warmth of their love flooded through her, filling her with an appreciation for all they'd been through to arrive at this point in their lives together, surrounded by the beauty of the vineyard.

This was a moment to cherish. Small moments like this meant more to her than grand gestures of love, although they had their share of those, too.

Bennett ran his hand along her cheek. "I'm sorry if I've been out of sorts. I've had a lot on my mind."

There it is, she thought. "City business?"

"It's always something, isn't it? But this weekend, it's just us, darling."

She smiled. "And quite a few friends."

"We can escape anytime we want," he said, drawing his hand down her back until her skin tingled with sweet memories. "I love you, Ivy. Maybe I haven't said that enough lately."

She pressed a finger to his warm lips. "I hear it every day, but more than that, I feel your love. I hope you can feel me loving you right back."

"Always," he murmured, his breath hot against her neck.

They lingered on the balcony for a few minutes, enjoying the feeling of being in each other's arms. Whatever issues they might have evaporated in their kisses.

Ivy's phone buzzed, and she groaned. She hated to answer it.

"It might be one of the girls," Bennett whispered against her neck.

"You're right," she said with a soft sigh. Even though Sunny and Misty were young adults now, they were always her children. She loved Bennett for understanding that.

She picked up her phone and answered it. "What's up, Shelly?"

"Where are you guys? You're missing the party."

"We're here, and we're changing."

"Okay, good. What are you wearing?"

"This isn't high school, Shells." Ivy chuckled while Bennett just smiled. "I brought my wine-colored dress. I thought I'd match my clothes to the wine, just in case I spill a glass."

Shelly's voice sounded tight. "You're not wearing that with Mom's pearls, are you?"

"That's a weird question, but no, I'm not. How many glasses of wine have you had?"

"Still on my first. I just wondered what happened to you, that's all."

"We'll see you soon," Ivy said lightly.

"I guess that's our signal to join the group," Bennett said, kissing her once more.

She changed into the flowing dress she'd brought. Made of a flattering jersey fabric, the style was chic in its simplicity and easy to wear. She picked up a thick twisted strand of garnets and rubellites her mother had acquired years ago on a buying trip to India for their import business.

"Need help with the clasp?" Bennett asked.

She swept her hair off her neck for him.

"I like your hair like that," he said, clasping the necklace before kissing her neck. "Will you wear it up tonight?"

She opened her bag and brought out a clip to hold her hair. "How's this?"

Bennett's approval shone in his eyes, not that she needed it, but she enjoyed it.

"You're beautiful," he said, kissing her again. "And this is the start to a beautiful weekend."

"It's nice to be guests for a change," she murmured. "We can pamper each other. Did you see the large bathtub?"

"I sure did," Bennett replied, his eyes sparkling.

They were back on track now, she thought with a happy feeling in her heart. After the renovation and the immediate rush of summer tourists at the inn, they both needed this respite. Perhaps her husband needed it more than she did.

Yet another reason not to concern him with her excavation project.

Once Ivy and Bennett were ready, they made their way toward the sounds of lively chatter. As they joined other guests on the bougainvillea-draped patio, Ivy spotted her sister in the crowd talking with Tristan and Emilie, who wore a long, understated black dress with a chunky necklace.

Wearing a vivid, bead-embroidered boho dress, Shelly waved them toward her and Mitch.

"I'm so glad you could join us," Tristan said, pouring glasses of wine for them. "This is one of our best vintages we reserve for special occasions. In this case, we're celebrating an excellent harvest that's well underway."

"You're harvesting now?" Ivy asked.

Emilie's face lit with a smile. "We started last week. This is turning out to be an excellent year. For most of our blocks of vines, harvest has been a little earlier than last year due to the weather. Only this area surrounding us remains, and it should be ready to pick next week."

"How do you know the right time?" Shelly asked.

"The berries tell us when they're ready," Tristan replied. "It's a natural process called *véraison*, when the grapes deepen into a dark reddish-purple color. The acidity declines and the natural sugars rise, so we test to determine the best time to harvest. Science and modern tools are our friends."

They raised their glasses and tasted the wine.

"This is incredible," Ivy said, enjoying the rich, dry flavor with elements of earthiness and spice.

Emilie put her nose to the glass and inhaled. "The climate and soil create an excellent *terroir*, so we're quite proud of this vintage. That was a very good year, and this year might be even better."

"Here's to an excellent harvest," Ivy said, raising her glass again.

Emilie gestured to a table that held a cornucopia of delicacies. "We also have an assortment of cheese, bread, pâté, and olives. Please help yourselves."

Shelly caught Ivy's eye and nodded across the patio. Not too far away, a younger, tattooed man approached the barn, his longish brown hair pulled back in a ponytail. He led a horse, stroking its neck and speaking to it as he walked.

Shelly raised her brow. "Horse whisperer?"

"Actually, he's the finest doctor around," Emilie said. "Excuse me, I should have a word with him before he leaves. We asked him to stay for the party, but he has another appointment. He's very much in demand."

Mitch asked Tristan a question about the winemaking process, and soon he and Bennett were immersed in conversation.

Several young women beside them noticed the doctor, too. Shelly nudged Ivy. "Looks like he's part of the show."

Ivy shot her a look and smiled at her sister's antics. "It wasn't that long ago you were one of those women. Not anymore."

Shelly tossed her hair back. "I'm married, not dead. I can still appreciate art in all its forms. My sweetie knows I'm all his."

Ivy leaned in toward her sister. "Do you know the big secret that Emilie and Tristan are planning for tonight?"

Shelly grinned. "I can't say, but I promise it's something you've never done before. Go with the flow, Ives. You'll love it."

When Ivy cast a look of concern toward Bennett, he simply shrugged, so she let it go.

3

Ivy circulated through the party with Bennett, chatting with old friends and meeting new people.

"Having a good time?" Bennett asked, tapping her glass.

"Wonderful," she replied. "It's good to see everyone here." She was sure that whatever Emilie and Tristan planned as a surprise for the evening would be fun.

The breeze carried aromatic scents from the vineyard and garden beyond the patio, along with the aroma of grilled seafood and barbecue. Just outside the area set up with dining tables was a wide vat of grapes from the recent harvest. She wondered what they would do with that.

All around them, guests were chatting and laughing. She and Bennett spoke with Carol Reston, the Grammy Award-winning singer, and her husband Hal. Indie film-makers Megan and Josh Calloway were also there. Megan filled her in on new research she'd discovered about Amelia in Switzerland for the documentary she'd been working on about her.

Bennett was deep in conversation with their friends when Mitch's phone buzzed.

He pulled it from his pocket. "Hey, Darla. What's up?" He paused and wrinkled his brow. "Are you sure?"

Immediately, a look of concern filled Shelly's face. "Is Daisy okay?"

Ivy pressed a hand to her sister's arm, hoping this wasn't anything serious.

Mitch raised a finger. "I thought Shelly brought the diaper bag in when we dropped off Daisy. Have you looked in the kitchen?"

"No, I thought you took it inside," Shelly said.

Mitch shook his head as he continued speaking with Darla. "If you've looked everywhere, it's probably not there. Maybe we forgot to bring it inside with us."

"We should go back," Shelly said, biting her lip. "Daisy needs her diapers and baby food and clothes. And her binky and panda. She'll be upset without them. I was afraid it was too early to leave her overnight."

"She'll be okay," Ivy said, trying to soothe her.

Mitch frowned at Shelly and went on. "She is? Sure, if you don't mind."

Growing agitated, Shelly reached for the phone. "I'll tell Darla we're leaving now."

"Sounds good. Thanks." Mitch tapped the phone and hung up. "Relax, babe. Darla has extras of everything there. She can call Louise to pick up anything she might need after the laundry closes."

Shelly pressed her fingers to her temple. "I wish I could've talked to Daisy. Is she upset?"

"Not at all." Mitch grinned. "She's happily eating berries. Darla is a pretty cool grandmother to Daisy. She's got this."

Ivy smiled and put an arm around her sister. "I know how hard it is to leave your baby girl alone the first time, but Daisy will be fine. Darla raised a son, remember?"

Slowly, Shelly nodded. "I just wanted Daisy to have everything she needed. What if she can't sleep in a strange house?"

"She knows Darla's place, and she can sleep anywhere now," Mitch said, kissing Shelly on the cheek.

When Shelly looked doubtful, Ivy said, "You can trust Darla to care for Daisy. She loves her and wouldn't let anything happen to her."

"I guess you're right," Shelly said, taking a sip from her glass.

A moment later, Emilie joined them again. Taking Shelly's hand with a wink, she said, "You should see my garden. Come with me."

"Go," Ivy said to Shelly with a reassuring look.

As Emilie led her away, Mitch turned back to Ivy. "Thanks for reassuring Shelly. She wanted to come, but I could tell that letting Daisy stay overnight was a big stretch for her. I didn't expect that. I miss the kiddo, too."

"It's another first," Ivy said, fondly recalling when her daughters were that age. Although her sister had always been spirited and carefree, she had grown into a concerned mother now.

A few minutes later, Ivy spied Shelly gripping her phone, so she started toward her.

Frowning, Shelly asked, "Be sure to get the right size diapers."

Ivy could hear Darla's gruff voice scratching over the phone. "If I run out, I'll pin a dishtowel on Daisy. I'm kidding, of course. Go have a good time."

Click.

Shelly stared at the phone. "I can't believe she hung up on me."

"That was the second call within ten minutes. Daisy will be fine. Darla and Poppy practically fought over who would babysit."

"I just wanted to tell Daisy good night."

"And did you?"

Shelly nodded with a little smile and slipped the phone into her purse.

"Time to return to the party, then." As she spoke, Ivy caught Bennett's eye across the tent and smiled. He was talking to Tristan and Mitch near a cluster of wine barrels.

As she and Shelly walked back to the patio, her heart went out to her sister. Ivy understood what she was going through.

Shelly sniffed. "You think I overreacted, don't you?"

"I think it's a natural reaction for your first overnight alone since Daisy was born."

"I trust Darla, but I was mad at myself and Mitch. Neither one of us remembered what was important for Daisy. I was so wrapped up in the plans for this weekend."

"We all make mistakes. Sounds like Darla is handling it, and Daisy is safe with her. Let it go."

"How did you manage with two kids?"

"Having children is like juggling. Sometimes you drop a ball, but you pick it up and keep going." Ivy hooked her arm through her sister's. "Crisis averted. Let's celebrate."

She steered Shelly toward the buffet tables arranged

under canvas sailcloth stretched overhead. Lanterns hung from posts, illuminating platters of crusty breads, assorted cheeses, and vegetables roasted with rosemary. The earthy, musky aroma of wooden wine barrels rose in the air.

"We'll feast tonight," Shelly said, relaxing as they sampled the cheeses. "Emilie said most everything came from their garden or other farms around here. She harvested the tomatoes this morning."

Ivy selected a fig wrapped in prosciutto, enjoying the fresh harvest and artisan creations.

As the sun sank toward the horizon, the clink of glasses punctuated conversations. A trio of musicians with a vocalist nearby began a soulful rendition of "La Vie en Rose," and several couples danced on the patio.

Hal and Carol chatted near the musicians. Her emerald silk outfit caught the light of a chandelier suspended overhead.

Ivy drank in the moment. After months of managing renovation crises and guests, being here was like surfacing for air. While Ivy loved managing the inn, this was rejuvenating.

Bennett joined her. He looked more like the man who'd wooed her on sunset beach walks than the mayor who'd spent the summer mediating disputes and planning budgets for the coming year.

With a soft squeeze of her shoulder, he asked, "Still enjoying yourself?"

"Even more now," she replied with a kiss. "Any idea what the surprise is?"

"Not a clue." Emilie signaled for everyone to move to the tables for the harvest celebration dinner, so Bennett took her hand.

The spirited conversations continued as they found their name cards and took their seats. Ivy and Bennett sat at a table with new faces, while Shelly and Mitch were at a table behind them.

The dinner began with the season's first pumpkin soup sprinkled with pepitas and swirled with herb-infused olive oil. Tristan opened more of their cherished wine from prior harvests to complement the grilled shrimp, barbecue, and vegan pasta they served. A salad consisting of late-summer tomatoes and cucumbers followed, along with a final course of cheese, fruit, and chocolate *pot de crème*.

After dinner, couples drifted to the dance floor again.

Bennett reached out to her. "Dance with me?"

"Always." She let him guide her through the other couples. Carol Reston sang one of her popular love songs, and Shelly and Mitch twirled past.

When the song ended, Tristan stepped forward. "We have a tradition here at Château Boivin for the harvest crush. We invite you to gather around the grape vat and the fire pit for a special surprise."

"This is it," Shelly whispered. "Get ready."

Outside the dining area, stars blanketed the vineyard, where old, twisted vines looked like an army of wrinkled gnomes in the moonlight.

The vat stood at the center of a circle of torches, their flames dancing in the light breeze. It was larger than Ivy had realized, reaching her shoulders, and the wood was worn smooth from years of use. Grapes filled it nearly to the brim. Deep purple clusters caught the firelight, gleaming like jewels, while the aroma rose thick and sweet in the night air.

Tristan stepped forward, grinning in a way that

suggested he'd been waiting all night for this moment. Emilie joined him, slipping her hand into his. The torchlight played across their faces.

"This is the highlight of our harvest crush," Tristan said, his voice carrying across the gathered crowd. "This year, we wanted to honor the old method of how wine used to be made in small villages."

Emilie's eyes sparkled. "Which means these grapes must be crushed. With the feet."

Tristan held up his arms and stomped the ground. "Who is brave enough to join us?"

Uneasy laughter rippled among the guests.

"We have togas inside," Emilie continued, gesturing toward the chateau. "It's good luck to crush the first grapes of the season."

Ivy laughed. "This reminds me of an old 'I Love Lucy' episode where Lucy and Ethel stomped grapes."

Several friends laughed and nodded while Emilie turned toward Ivy, her gaze landing on her and Bennett. "I think I know who our first volunteers should be."

At once, Ivy realized what Shelly and Emilie had planned. She clasped Bennett's hand for strength.

Emilie smiled. "Tradition usually calls for the youngest maidens, but we'll make exceptions tonight. Who'll be our first volunteers? How about the mayor?"

The crowd started chanting his name.

Raising his hand, Bennett shook his head. "I think there are more deserving people here. Mitch, how about you?"

But their friends kept up the chant.

Realizing the inevitable plan was afoot, Ivy tucked her arm through her husband's. She wouldn't let him do this alone. "Come on, Mr. Mayor. Let's show them how it's done."

Bennett's eyebrows shot up. "You're serious."

"I don't think we have a choice," she said.

She squeezed his arm, feeling a little giddy and reckless in a way she hadn't in ages. Maybe it was the wine, or the end of the summer's demands, or just the sheer absurdity of being invited to stomp grapes in a wooden vat under the stars.

"We're sleeping here tonight anyway," she said. "No driving, no responsibilities. Just us and a vat full of grapes."

Shelly grabbed Ivy's hand. "Come on, when was the last time we did anything outrageous?"

The crowd cheered. Emilie clapped her hands together, delighted. "Let's go get ready."

The four of them followed Emilie to the house. Inside a room off the kitchen, the air smelled of dried lavender that hung from the beams. Emilie gestured to a rack of white sheets fashioned into togas.

The linen was soft and worn thin in places, carrying the subtle scent of lavender. "Last year these were Halloween ghost costumes, and tonight they're our togas. Ivy, here's one for you."

Emilie demonstrated the wrapping technique with practiced efficiency, pinning the sheet at one shoulder and gathering it at the waist with another strip of cloth.

Tristan had already changed. He was tall, and his toga ended just above his knees. "Be sure to put your swimsuits underneath."

With relief, Ivy saw that Emilie had laid out their swimsuits for them. At least they'd have that.

"I can't believe we're doing this," Bennett said, chuckling.

Mitch elbowed him. "Think of the photos, dude."

They changed in minutes with more laughter than skill. Bennett struggled with his toga until Ivy fixed it for him. The sheet was cool against her skin. Shelly emerged from the other room looking excited with her hair pinned up and her feet bare.

Shelly grinned. "Aren't you glad you got that pedicure now?"

They filed back outside to whoops and applause. The torches burned brightly, throwing flickering shadows across the vat. They sat down on a wooden bench beside buckets of water.

"And now for the ceremonial foot washing," Emilie said. She splashed water over everyone's feet.

When they were all cleaned and dried, Tristan gestured toward the vat. A wooden ladder leaned against its side, the rungs worn smooth.

Carol Reston's voice rose above the rest. "Show us how it's done, Mr. Mayor."

Bennett shot Ivy a look that said, "This was your idea," before climbing the ladder with exaggerated dignity. The toga billowed around his legs. At the top, he paused, peering down into the purple mass below. The torchlight flickered across his face, catching the uncertainty there before he masked it with a grin.

"Here goes." He stepped in.

The wet crunch made guests laugh. Bennett's expression shifted to surprise as his feet sank ankle-deep into fruit.

He chuckled and reached for Ivy. "Don't leave me in here alone."

Ivy eyed the vat, having second thoughts. She glanced at Tristan. "Is this sanitary? You're not actually going to use these grapes for wine, are you?"

Tristan appeared at her elbow, grinning. "No, no. Don't worry. These are leftovers from the harvest. It's tradition. You see, the Romans believed crushing the first grapes with bare feet brought good fortune for the vintage. Mostly it's just fun."

Bennett braced himself against the vat's rim, testing his balance. Grape skins clung to his calves. "Your turn, sweetheart."

Ivy hesitated on the ladder.

Bennett reached for her, swooping her into his arms and lifting her over the edge, then lowering her into the vat.

She gasped as her feet hit the grapes. The fruit gave way like wet sand, cold and slick, and she sank past her ankles. The sensation shot up her legs as grapes collapsed under her weight. Juice seeped between her toes, and she grabbed Bennett's shoulders to keep from slipping.

"Oh, my gosh." She couldn't stop laughing. "This is wild."

Bennett tried to shift his weight, but his foot slid sideways. He caught himself on the vat's edge, his knuckles white against the stained wood.

Laughing, Ivy helped him up, cool pulp squelching with every tiny movement. She found very little solid ground, just layers and layers of slippery fruit.

The crowd howled with laughter and cheered them on.

Ivy waved to Shelly and Mitch. "You have to come in."

She clung to Bennett as he attempted a step. His leg disappeared to mid-calf and emerged dripping. Purple stains crept up their shins.

Emilie climbed the ladder with the confidence of one who'd done this before. She gathered her toga, stepped in, and waded toward them like she was crossing a shallow stream.

"You have to keep moving," Emilie called over the music. Her feet made soft crushing sounds with each step. "If you stand still too long, you sink."

Shelly and Mitch were laughing so hard they could hardly climb the ladder.

Tristan followed Emilie. They formed an unsteady circle with Ivy and Bennett, each of them gripping another's shoulder for balance. The grapes shifted constantly beneath them.

"Ready?" Tristan raised a hand. "Let's crush it!"

They began to stomp to the music.

It was chaos. The grapes burst and sprayed, and juice spattered their togas. Ivy lifted her knees high, trying to find a rhythm. Bennett laughed and nearly went down again.

Shelly and Mitch were at the top of the ladder, laughing at them.

Ivy nodded to her sister. "You got us into this, so you'd better join us."

"We're coming," Mitch said. He scooped an arm under Shelly's legs and stepped to the vat's edge.

Their friends roared their approval.

With her arms wrapped around Mitch's neck, Shelly laughed. "Woo-hoo, here we come. Don't you dare drop me."

With Shelly clinging to him, Mitch mounted the ladder one-handed. At the top, he paused, adjusting his grip, and stepped in.

Ivy saw the exact moment he misjudged the weight distribution.

Still holding Shelly, Mitch came down on a particularly slick patch of pulverized grapes. His feet shot out from under him, and Shelly screamed.

They hit with a tremendous splash that sent grapes splattering in all directions.

Shelly shrieked as Mitch disappeared under the purple mass.

Ivy and the rest of them stumbled, grabbing the vat's rim for support. They all dissolved with laughter as their friends cheered them on, capturing the action in photos and videos.

Mitch surfaced first, spitting grape skins, his toga plastered to his chest. Grape pulp clung to his hair and eyebrows, and his blond hair was purple now.

Shelly was beside him, gasping and laughing. She tried to stand and immediately slipped again, catching herself on Mitch's shoulder.

"You dropped me," she said, grinning.

"I slipped, babe." Mitch wiped his eyes, smearing more juice across his face. "There's no traction in here. It's like ice skating in fruit."

Their friends had gone wild, cheering and whistling. Someone started a new chant, though Ivy couldn't make out the words over the music. Her stomach ached from laughing.

Emilie waded toward them, somehow managing to look graceful even hip-deep in crushed grapes. "You're such a good sport. This is why we asked you to bring swimsuits and stay overnight. After we clean up, we'll relax in the hot tub."

"Thank goodness for that," Ivy said, chuckling. "I had no idea we were going to be the entertainment. What a blast, though."

Next to her, Bennett was stomping with full commitment now. The vat trembled under their combined movement.

Shelly gave up standing. Instead, she sat waist-deep in the grapes, howling with laughter, while Mitch attempted to pull her upright. Every time he got her halfway up, his feet would slip, and they'd collapse again into a fresh explosion of fruit.

"Come on," Tristan called over the music. "Let's finish with style."

They all helped Shelly and Mitch stand and formed a ragged circle. They managed to stomp sort of in unison to the music for nearly a minute.

Ivy couldn't remember when she'd had so much fun.

Their friends cheered and cameras flashed. Carol Reston had claimed a prime spot near the torches, directing video angles like she was staging a production. Ivy caught a glimpse of her own shadow, looking like a giant figure dancing in a vat of grapes.

The absurdity of it hit her again. She was stomping grapes in a makeshift toga while people filmed the mayor of Summer Beach doing the same thing. This would be all over social media by morning.

She didn't care at all.

Her feet found rhythm in the chaos, and Bennett's hand found hers. Their skin was sticky with pulp.

"We did it, sweetheart." He squeezed her hand and raised it overhead in victory.

Someone in the crowd whistled.

Emilie directed them to cluster at the vat's center. "Everyone together now. Let's get the final photos."

They pressed close, arms around shoulders, trying not to slip. The grapes shifted beneath them. Ivy felt Bennett's strong arms around her as Shelly clung to her on the other side for dear life.

Ivy tilted her face skyward. Stars pierced the darkness above, more visible here than in Summer Beach, away from the coastal fog and town lights. The Milky Way stretched overhead.

This is living in the moment, she thought, filled with happiness.

Bennett turned his face to hers. "I love you for going along with this."

"I couldn't let you have all the fun." She laughed and kissed him, tasting grapes on his lips.

"Time to shower," Emilie called out. "This way, *allons-y.*"

Tristan offered strong hands to help them up and out. Ivy's legs trembled as she gripped the rungs. Whether from exertion or laughter or too much wine, she couldn't tell. Her feet left purple prints on each wooden step.

"The outdoor showers are this way," Emilie said, leading them around the side of the house. Fresh robes hung on hooks nearby.

Ivy and Bennett peeled off their togas and sprayed each other off in their swimsuits, still chuckling at the absurdity of what they'd done and the unexpected fun. They slipped into the plush robes provided and strolled to the hot tub.

The party was breaking up, with the rest of the guests staying on the property making their way to their rooms and cottages.

Ivy eased into the foaming hot water beside Bennett. "That was the most fun I've had in months."

Across from them, Shelly climbed in next to Mitch. Grinning, she added, "You needed to let loose a little, Ives. Didn't I tell you it would be fun?"

Bennett pulled Ivy close. "What a way to start a new season."

"That was awesome, dude." Mitch positioned himself by a jet. "The only question is how, do we top that for Thanksgiving?"

Ivy splashed her sister. "We'll find a way, won't we, Shells?"

4

*L*ater that evening, after bathing and washing her hair to get the last of the grapes out, Ivy slipped into a silky gown and robe. She joined Bennett on a small sofa in front of the fireplace in their room.

She let out a contented sigh. "I've been thinking about what you said about the season. The inn feels different now. It's the first time we haven't had a long list of repairs to do in the off-season."

Bennett stroked his stubbled chin. "Do you miss the chaos?"

She shrugged. "Maybe a little."

"Sometimes I feel the same way. You achieved a big goal. The challenge and constant activity kept every day fresh."

"We had a lot of surprises. Not all pleasant, but in retrospect, we can laugh about it now."

Bennett put his arm around her and drew her close. "It's awfully quiet there now."

She tucked her feet under her, thinking about the

season ahead. "We should plan a big feast for Thanksgiving. That's one of my favorite holidays. It's about feeling gratitude and spending time with loved ones and friends."

"Before the Christmas open house? That's a lot of work for you."

"Still, I'd like to do something special. Maybe we should create another tradition." She had an idea in mind. "What about families in need in Summer Beach?"

Bennett nodded thoughtfully. "Sadly, there are always some. If we know about the situation, community organizations try to help."

Ivy stared into the fire, thinking about what they could contribute. She made a mental note to establish a food drop-off point at the inn for less fortunate families.

Thanksgiving was one of her favorite holidays, though it was recognized only in the United States and Canada, which celebrated with a feast several weeks earlier.

First embraced by ancestors who settled in New England hundreds of years ago, the harvest celebration was originally derived from those of Indigenous tribes, including the Wampanoag, that had long honored harvests with feasts of thanksgiving.

Ivy recalled that the modern version of the celebration was put forth by Sarah Josepha Hale to bring the United States together post-Civil War. In the nineteenth century, Hale also published "Mary Had a Little Lamb," helped establish Vassar College, and advocated for women's education and rights as property owners.

This year, Ivy and her family would celebrate by giving thanks for their family and friends and hosting a harvest feast.

"I wish Misty could make it home for the holiday." The

words came out more wistful than she intended, so she tried to inject brightness into her tone. "Though I know she's busy with her career."

"Has she booked anything new?"

Ivy nodded, her spirit lifting with pride. "Yesterday, she called with news that she had landed a part in a film shooting in New Zealand. Another actor took ill. It's a small part, but she's thrilled."

"That's wonderful." Bennett shifted to look at her. "When does it shoot?"

"November." The word sat heavy between them. Enjoying the warmth of the fire, Ivy watched the logs crackle. "So, no Thanksgiving for her this year."

Bennett traced small circles on her shoulder with his fingers. He didn't say anything, just waited.

"I know it's her career," Ivy continued. She could hear the forced reasonableness in her voice. "This is what she's worked for. And she has her life in Los Angeles. I can't expect her to drop everything for one meal."

"But you miss her."

"Of course, I do."

The simple observation cracked open her heart, and Ivy's throat tightened. "Parents want their children to grow up and follow their dreams. You think those young years will last forever, but in the grand scheme of life, it's only a few years. Then you live the rest of your life without them. Missing them."

"Until the grandkids arrive."

"Maybe, maybe not."

The possibility of that seemed a long way off to Ivy, and she didn't want to pressure her daughters to marry or have children. She might hope for that, but most of all, she wanted them to follow their dreams and live a good life.

"What did you and your family do for Thanksgiving?" Ivy asked.

"I always went to my sister's house," he replied. "Even when Jackie was alive. What about you? What did you do when the girls were young?"

"We were all crammed into a small kitchen. Misty would complain about the heat in the kitchen, and Sunny would steal bites of everything before it was done." She swallowed against the bittersweet memories of Jeremy. "It all ended so suddenly."

Bennett understood because his first wife had died, just as her husband had. Their marriage was a second chance for each of them.

"Life has its seasons," he said. "Children grow up and build their own lives. That's what's supposed to happen. Doesn't mean the love is any less."

She blinked against the emotion filling her eyes. "I'm happy for her. Really. This is everything she's wanted."

Bennett pulled her closer, and she rested her cheek against his shoulder.

"You're allowed to be disappointed," he said softly. "Being happy for her doesn't mean you can't have coexisting emotions."

Ivy exhaled. He was right, of course. The Thanksgiving she'd been imagining this year with everyone gathered at the inn and a big harvest table laden with food would be missing pieces of her heart.

Her parents were still sailing around the world on their boat, so they wouldn't be there. Instead, they would be navigating their way around the Cape of Good Hope just south of Cape Town in South Africa.

Misty was following her dream of an acting career, one that she'd studied and worked so diligently for.

Bennett was right about coexisting emotions. Ivy was disappointed that she wouldn't see them for the holiday but happy that those she loved were following their dreams.

Misty telling stories about auditions, Sunny rolling her eyes, and all of them together wouldn't happen this year. Maybe never again in the same way. Sunny would be the next to leave. These were the empty nest years people warned about. Find a hobby or volunteer, they advised.

In her case, her nest was filled with guests at the inn. They'd fill their harvest table with others this year.

Still, she could hope.

"Maybe Misty can come home for Christmas," Ivy said. "Is that too much to ask the universe?"

Bennett pressed a kiss to her cheek. "That's never stopped you before. Ask for anything you can dream of. But remember why Misty and your parents won't be with us this year."

"I know, and I want the best for them, just as they do for me. That means we're not always walking or sailing the same path, but it's sweet when our paths cross."

Still, she sent up her silent wishes on plumes of smoke.

Staring into the crackling fire, she tried to minimize her disappointment and concentrate on the positive pursuits of her parents and Misty. Relaxing in front of the fireplace with Bennett, wrapped in his arms, life seemed more manageable.

"We'll make this year a celebration of what the year has

brought us," Bennett said. "And share it with others. That's what we do in Summer Beach."

"The holidays at the inn are different," Ivy said thoughtfully. She recalled guests they'd had in years past, those who'd appeared with gifts of the spirit they hadn't known they needed.

This was the season of harvest, the time to reap what had been planted. "I wonder if we planted enough goodwill to harvest this year?"

Bennett chuckled. "Every crop grows better with fertilizer. With the renovation, you certainly had your share of manure, so to speak."

Though Ivy laughed at his joke, she still had a prickly feeling that this year's harvest season might serve up the unexpected.

5

*B*ennett braced his foot against the side of Mitch's boat, testing the tension on the rope he'd just secured. The dock swayed beneath them, responding to the gentle roll of the harbor. Overhead, white seagulls circled and called.

"That should hold." Bennett brushed off his deck shoes and straightened, wiping his palms on his khaki shorts. "When did this cleat start pulling loose?"

"Last charter trip. I noticed it when we were cruising the coastline." Mitch ran his hand along the hull, checking the repair. "This boat keeps threatening retirement, but we're not there yet."

The craft showed its age in the weathered trim and faded deck paint, but everything else reflected careful maintenance. Bennett had been aboard enough times to know Mitch treated the vessel like family. Regular upkeep, prompt repairs, nothing deferred.

"How does she handle with a full group?" Bennett asked.

"Steady and comfortable." Mitch moved toward the stern, inspecting another cleat. "The small cabins below make overnight trips possible, like runs to Catalina Island. Even the Channel Islands. People want experiences now, not just a sunset cruise."

Bennett followed him. They'd all returned from the crush just a couple of days ago. "Speaking of experiences, any more on the vandalism at Java Beach?"

Mitch glanced back at him. "The Polynesian beach scene on the side wall is completely trashed. Jagged black paint streaks across the whole mural. Have you seen it yet?"

"When I went for my run this morning. Looks like you tried to clean it off."

Mitch's jaw tightened. "Shelly and I scrubbed it some when we got back from the vineyard, but it was useless. The whole thing needs to be redone."

"I'm sorry, man." Bennett shook his head. "Any idea who did it?"

"None. Happened sometime after closing and before Ginger's book club ended." Mitch picked up the wrench and turned it over in thought. "Most of the chairs and tables I put out there for customers were okay. Two chairs were broken, but they can be repaired."

Bennett watched the water lap against the hull, considering his next words. "I was at Nailed It earlier, and Jen mentioned that she and George caught something on the hardware store's security camera."

Mitch looked up sharply. "I saw they called, but I haven't gotten back to them. What did they see?"

"Someone walking around the corner of your building toward the beach during the time you said it happened."

Bennett crossed his arms. "Looked like a skinny guy with jeans and a dark hoodie with something printed on the back. Couldn't make out the face. The camera angle was wrong, but the build suggested a teenager, maybe early twenties."

"Half the guys around here fit that description, including me, but that's more than we had before." Mitch set down the wrench. "Did they give that to Clark?"

"Jen gave it to the police officers. They're working on it." Bennett hesitated. "I might have an idea who it is."

"Yeah?"

"My morning runs take me through town around six. For the past couple of weeks, I've seen a young guy matching that description. Similar hoodie, dark with faded lettering across the back. Can't quite read it, but it's there. He's always alone, walking with his hands shoved into his pockets like he's trying not to be noticed."

Bennett had been watching him, and something about the guy made him think of Mitch when he'd first seen him at the beach years ago. The young man had been on his mind lately, and this was disturbing Bennett.

Mitch frowned. "Where does he hang out?"

"Different spots. Sometimes near the marina. Once by the public restrooms at the beach access. Yesterday, I saw him sitting on a bench near the library lot." Bennett rubbed the back of his neck. "He's got that look. Unwashed hair, same clothes. My guess is he's homeless or a runaway. Probably both."

Mitch looked out at the horizon. "Kind of like I was."

Bennett didn't need to say anything. When he'd discovered Mitch all those years ago, he was just released from prison but also determined to make a fresh start. He was brewing coffee and selling it on the beach to the morning surfers.

"Do you think he's in trouble?" Mitch asked.

"I can't tell. He doesn't seem like he's on drugs, and he doesn't seem to be in a hurry to leave."

Mitch's anger seemed to deflate, and concern filled his eyes. "He might be staying at the shelter or looking for work."

"Possibly. They don't have many beds, so he could be sleeping on the beach. There are spots in the coves where someone could camp without being obvious. I haven't seen him since last week."

"I feel kind of bad for him," Mitch said quietly. "Still, if he wrecked my mural and destroyed property, that's not okay. But if he's homeless or running from trouble, that's another story." He trailed off, continuing to stare in thought. "There's a reason people lash out like that. Usually, they're hurt or angry."

"Doesn't make it right."

"No, but it's understandable." Mitch picked up his toolbox, sliding it toward the dock. "The artist who painted the original mural is Carmella. She paints murals all over Southern California and got her start as a graffiti artist. I'm not saying that was right, but she's talented and learned her craft. Now she paints a lot of murals. Anyway, my regulars at Java Beach set up a fund to pay her to repaint it, and they've already raised enough. So that's taken care of. Carmella can use the work, so in a funny way, it's a win."

Bennett lifted a corner of his mouth. "The community sure shows up for you."

Mitch climbed onto the dock, offering Bennett a hand up. "Doesn't mean I wasn't disappointed about the vandalism when it happened. But at least the place wasn't robbed or the kitchen smashed up."

They secured the boat, double-checking lines before gathering their tools. The afternoon sun hung low over the water. A few other boat owners worked on their vessels nearby, calling out greetings as Bennett and Mitch headed from the marina.

Bennett was reaching for his keys when Mitch stopped abruptly.

"Hey, is that the dude?"

Bennett followed his gaze. Walking along the marina access road, head down and shoulders hunched, was the guy. Same dark hoodie with faded lettering. Same jeans, torn at the knees. Same defeated posture.

"That's him," Bennett said softly.

They exchanged a look. Mitch set down his toolbox by the vehicle. "Let's talk to him."

They approached carefully, not wanting to spook the kid into running. Bennett took the lead, keeping his voice neutral and non-threatening.

"Hey, buddy. Excuse me."

The kid froze, eyes darting between them like he was calculating escape routes. Up close, Bennett saw he was younger than expected. Sixteen, maybe seventeen. Gaunt cheeks. Dark circles under wary eyes.

"I didn't do anything," the kid said automatically.

"Didn't say you did." Bennett stopped a few feet away, keeping his posture open. "Just want to talk to see if you need help. I'm Bennett Dylan. We're not cops."

"I know who you are." The kid's voice carried an edge. "You're the mayor. Saw you in the paper."

Bennett gestured toward Mitch. "And this is Mitch Kline. He owns Java Beach, the coffee shop."

Something flickered across the kid's face, maybe guilt, but he masked it quickly. "So?"

"Someone vandalized Mitch's place a couple nights ago. Spray-painted the mural on the side wall and broke some furniture."

The kid's jaw tightened. "That doesn't mean it was me."

"You're right. It doesn't." Mitch stepped forward, his voice gentler than Bennett expected. "It's cool, though. The artist is going to repaint it. You know, when I landed in Summer Beach, I was kind of lost and hungry. Now that I have my coffee shop, I usually make more food than I need. Some of the surfers chasing the waves stop by. I'm usually in the kitchen, and there's a back door. Come anytime you're hungry."

"I don't need help." The words came out defensive, brittle. "I'm fine."

"Are you?" Bennett asked. "Because from where I'm standing, you look like someone who's been sleeping rough and hasn't had a decent meal in days. Maybe you left home, and maybe you had good reason."

The kid's eyes went glassy. He blinked hard, looking away. "I didn't mean to," he began, then stopped.

"Listen, dude," Mitch said, lowering his voice. "If you did it, you need to own that sometime. But I think you're hurting. And I'd rather help you than throw you to the cops. I know what the inside of a cell looks like. It ain't pretty."

The kid stared at them with raw desperation in his eyes. For a moment, Bennett thought he might confess and let them help him.

Then his expression shuttered. "I have to go."

He turned and hurried off, not quite running but close. Bennett started to follow, but Mitch caught his arm.

"Let him go."

They watched the kid disappear around the corner toward a beach path.

Bennett pulled out his phone. "I'll call Clark and tell him we just talked to the kid. Maybe the police can track him down before he bolts."

Mitch shook his head. "I think he's scared. Do you need to make that call right now?"

"This puts me in a tough spot. I should."

"I won't press charges."

Bennett sighed. "I still need to make the call."

Mitch drew a hand over his jaw. "I'll bet that was a grainy video. Could have been anyone with jeans and a hoodie. Heck, I looked like that when I was his age. But you do what you need to do."

Bennett dialed Clark's number. The phone rang twice before the police chief answered. Bennett turned away, lowering his voice as he explained what just happened.

He stood by the marina railing, looking out at the boats rocking gently in their slips. "I've seen this kid around, but I can't be sure he was the one in the video Jen showed me. Might be one of the surfers passing through. They're usually harmless. Maybe Brother Rip has seen him around."

The dreadlocked pastor served locals and itinerant surfers, often surfing with them in the morning and afternoon when the waves were good. He also officiated at beach weddings, including Bennett and Ivy's.

After speaking with the chief and hanging up, he turned back to Mitch. "I did what I could."

"Thanks, man. I hope he stops by the kitchen. I feel bad that I didn't even ask his name. I'd like to hear his story."

Mitch's compassion was touching, especially since Bennett knew what he'd been through. "Maybe he will."

6

___

"How about a wine tasting?" Shelly suggested, tapping her pencil at the desk in the foyer. "Emilie and Tristan want to visit anyway, and they could sell their wine."

"I forgot to mention that we agreed on a wine tasting week in the new year," Ivy replied. "But they might like to join us for our Thanksgiving celebration, unless they have other plans. I'll ask them."

Even though several days had passed, Ivy still thought about the magical weekend she'd shared at the vineyard with her family and friends. The couple enjoyed visiting while their vines were sleeping in the winter.

However, Ivy couldn't afford to let the inn sleep in the off-season. To many travelers, this was the best time to visit Summer Beach. Crowds were thinner, and the beach was generally sunny. A light jacket was all people needed to make the transition from summer days to cool autumn evenings.

Every year, their challenge was how to let people know

that autumn was still a great time to visit the beach. Ivy reviewed the reservations on the screen at the front desk. They needed more ideas, especially given they'd been closed for the renovation this year.

Shelly snapped her fingers. "What about a cooking week? We've had good luck with those before."

"Or a spa week," Sunny added, rounding the corner. "People would need that after a week of cooking. I was wrapping up homework on the computer, and I heard you talking in the office."

Ivy appreciated the input from her daughter, but there was a catch. "Those courses depend on who we can get to teach them. Any ideas?"

Shelly shook her head. "I'd offer Mitch for a cooking week, but he's pretty busy at Java Beach now that one of his part-timers went back to school."

Sunny spoke up again. "What about that cookbook author who stayed here? Even though I don't cook, I love watching videos of her making dishes on her social channels. She's all about the fusion of flavors."

"Diya Donnelly," Ivy said. "Those chai cookies she brought with her last year were amazing. I'll call her. Good idea, Sunny."

The compliment lit Sunny's smile. "Thanks, Mom. I've got to go to class now."

Her daughter was taking extra classes at the university now. She slid her laptop into her backpack, twisted her strawberry blond hair into a knot, and left for school.

Just then, the front door creaked softly. When it swung open, Ivy flicked her eyes up and hesitated, taking in the younger man who stood before her.

Oddly, she'd seen him before. A memory flashed through her mind.

The horse whisperer.

With dark-lashed blue eyes, a muscular build, and tattoos covering his arms, this man filled the room with his presence. A fluffy white Australian Shepherd beside him stared up at Ivy with alert eyes.

She tried to recall what Emilie said about him. *A doctor,* that was it.

Behind the polished antique reservation desk, Shelly nudged her.

Ivy ignored her sister, though she wondered what the man's story was and why he was here. She cleared her throat. "Welcome to the Seabreeze Inn."

The sound of the surf drew his attention, and his gaze drifted through open windows. "Looks like a great day to catch waves out there."

"Sure is," Shelly said, a mischievous smile on her lips. "Hope you brought your swimsuit."

A grin crossed his face. "This time of year, I think I'd need a wetsuit. I'm Caleb Montana. I reserved a pet-friendly room."

Ivy tapped the reservation screen, ignoring another jab from Shelly. "I see your reservation, Dr. Montana. We have a room for you in our Sunset suites behind the main house."

Ivy began the registration process while Shelly fished out an old-fashioned key. They still used these, even after the renovation they'd just completed. The inn still retained the flavor and charm of a grand, century-old beach house, just with working plumbing and electricity, much to Ivy's relief.

Ivy looked up. "And who is this with you?"

Caleb looked down with admiration at his canine companion. "This is Starry. She found me on a camping trip when she was a pup. The stars overhead were amazing that night, and when I spun around, it reminded me of a van Gogh."

"*Starry Night*, right?" Ivy recalled seeing the Vincent van Gogh painting at the Museum of Modern Art in New York City.

Caleb grinned. "Yeah, at MoMA. So that's how she got her name. Don't worry, she's friendly."

Ivy held out her hand, and Starry inched forward to sniff it. The dog's tail began to wag, and she licked Ivy's hand.

Caleb nodded his approval. "She seems to like you. Do you have any dogs?"

Before Ivy could answer, footsteps creaked on the stairway behind them. Glancing up, Ivy saw their long-term resident descending.

Gilda was a magazine feature writer who often kept to herself, except for volunteering at Thrifty Threads, a secondhand shop that supports animal rescue and helps find new homes for abandoned pets. Her pink-tinted hair glistened in the sunlight flooding the entryway, and she carried a small Chihuahua in her arms.

At the sight of Starry, the little dog's ears perked up, and she fairly vibrated with excitement.

Gilda laughed. "Pixie wanted to go downstairs, and now I see why. She loves big dogs and thinks she's one of them, don't you, sweetikins?"

Starry lifted her nose to Pixie, acknowledging her with

keen interest and a wag of her tail. Still, Starry remained by Caleb's side.

However, a split second later, Pixie wriggled free of Gilda's grasp and leapt, sailing through the air like a fearless hang glider—only without the glider.

"No, no, baby!" Stretching her arms toward Pixie, Gilda stumbled on the stair. She grabbed the railing to stop her fall.

Shelly cried out in horror, but she was too far from Pixie. "Catch her!"

Ivy couldn't move fast enough, but Caleb dove for the tiny dog in a flash. Unfortunately, he fell short, hitting the floor with a thud.

Pixie landed with a thud just out of his grasp, her front leg buckling on impact. An anguished screech split the air.

Horrified, Ivy rushed to help Pixie, and they all gathered around the poor little creature.

"Oh, my baby," Gilda said, tears filling her eyes. As she scooped Pixie in her arms, the little dog cried out in pain again.

Caleb pushed himself from the floor. "I don't like the sound of that. May I look at her?"

When Gilda looked doubtful, Shelly added quickly, "It's okay. He's a doctor."

Ivy wondered what he could do for the little dog. "There's an animal hospital in the next town. It's not far from here."

"I know right where it is," he said.

With a gentle touch, Caleb inspected Pixie's front leg while the little dog whined. "She has pain and instability in the leg. It appears to be fractured, though it's a closed fracture, meaning the skin isn't punctured. That's good. I'll get my bag and put a temporary splint on this leg. She'll need X-rays to determine the extent of her injury."

He paused and turned to his canine companion before leaving. "Starry, stay. Stay with Pixie while I'm gone."

The fluffy white dog stretched out beside Gilda and licked Pixie's face in comfort.

Pixie quieted, and Gilda let out a breath. "It all happened so fast."

Shelly shook her head. "As things do, poor baby."

"Where did the doctor come from?" Gilda asked.

Shelly twisted her lips to one side. "My money is on Mount Olympus or the Mr. Universe competition. Did you see his arms? He didn't get those from lifting a stethoscope."

Ivy blew a wisp of hair from her eyes in exasperation. "You're incorrigible. And very married."

Shelly shrugged. "I still have an eye for artistic form. I'm just window shopping for my single besties. You know I always help my friends."

Ivy rubbed her side. "You were jabbing me so hard, he'll have to treat me for broken ribs next."

Caleb hurried through the open door. After opening a black bag, he withdrew some supplies. "I'll stabilize this leg, so she doesn't sustain further injury." He looked up at Gilda with a sympathetic smile. "She'll be okay. You can hold her and ride with me if you want."

Gilda turned to Ivy. "Would you get her favorite blanket for me?"

"I'll be right back." With her heart still racing from the incident, Ivy dashed upstairs to Gilda's room. She found a small pillow that had disappeared from the living room last month, but she decided to leave that in the dog bed. She returned with Pixie's blanket and a couple of soft toys from her dog bed.

Caleb worked quickly and then walked with Gilda to his SUV. Starry trotted protectively behind them.

Shelly leaned against the door, wiping her eyes as she watched them go. "Poor little Pixie."

Ivy was touched at Shelly's sudden emotion. "Dr. Montana seemed confident she'll pull through."

Shelly sniffed. "As annoying as that little kleptomaniac dog is, I love her. She's one of us."

Ivy put her arm around her sister. "Doggie therapy hasn't helped Pixie much. I found that missing seashell pillow from the living room in her bed. But she's ours. She's been here almost from the beginning."

From the night of the Ridgetop Fire, Ivy recalled, when they welcomed local refugees from the ridge, including Bennett.

Shelly managed a weak grin. "If the doctor were thirty years older, that would have been the perfect meet-cute for Gilda. He seems to know what he's doing around dogs. Do you think Pixie will come back with a cute little cast we can sign?"

Heaving a sigh, Ivy said, "What am I going to do with you?"

"The question is, what are we going to do with him? I'm betting on Sunny to fall for him. She took the reservation. Too bad she just missed him."

Ivy swatted her. "Don't set anyone up for a broken heart. He's just passing through town."

Poppy came through the rear carrying bags of supplies. "When I drove by the front, I saw Gilda getting into an

SUV with Pixie and a guy who looked like a tattooed body-builder. What's going on?"

They quickly filled her in.

"I hope Pixie will be okay. She's like a member of the family."

Shelly drummed her fingers on the desk. "In the meantime, do you think it's safe to go digging for buried treasure yet?"

Ivy shrugged a shoulder. "We need to do that in the daylight this time, so I should tell Forrest and Bennett."

"I could talk to Dad," Poppy began.

"No, I can handle our brother," Shelly said, making a face. "He can't say no to his little sister."

"His spoiled little sister." Ivy grinned. They'd all doted on Shelly by the time she came along. She was like a baby doll they dressed up and played with.

Shelly turned to Ivy. "How do you plan to get Bennett on board?"

"I didn't say I was asking for permission," Ivy replied. "I don't need it, but I should show him the courtesy of telling him what we're up to this time."

"So we don't get arrested," Poppy said, excitement filling her face.

"Or draw a lot of nosy neighbors." Ivy paused. "Shelly, you get to tell Darla."

Shelly sliced the air with her hands. "No way. I'm drawing the line at that. Or maybe I'll tell her we're breaking ground on a community garden until we're ready to build. That's a good story for her."

Ivy stared at her. "Actually, that's a good idea."

"You really think she'll believe it?" Shelly arched an eyebrow.

"No, I meant we should do something like that," Ivy said, her mind turning. "It's good for kids to learn how to cultivate food. I think a lot of people would be interested in a community garden. I only wish it could be permanent."

Having studied horticulture and managing gardens at the inn, Shelly brightened. "Oh, my gosh, yes. The town needs that. Is there room on the land?"

Ivy tried to recall the placement. "I don't know. I'd have to ask Forrest."

"I'll do that," Shelly said. Grinning, she held up her hands. "Let's do this next week. I can't wait to say, 'Ladies, start your shovels.'"

They all laughed, though Ivy was serious about this potential new project. A community garden might be just as intriguing as whatever was buried under there.

7

___

As Ivy made her way to the kitchen in the morning, she wondered if she'd misread Bennett earlier.

Poppy passed her with a basket of muffins on her way to the dining room. "Guests sure are thirsty this morning. Would you start another pot of coffee?"

"Will do," Ivy replied. In the kitchen, she measured out the coffee and punched the start button on the coffeemaker. While the machine gurgled to life, she cleaned the counters and put up the dishes, her thoughts still on Bennett.

Maybe she was reading something into his quiet behavior this week. She didn't expect him to tell her everything that was going on in the community. This probably didn't concern her, but if it troubled Bennett, then that was her business.

Poppy pushed the door open and glanced at the coffeemaker. "Are you still going to the farmers market today?"

"Soon. Is there anything you need?"

"If you see any baby artichokes, could you pick up a

few? I'm not sure they're still in season, but Mitch promised to show me how to make them grilled and crispy."

Ivy never knew what she'd find at the Saturday morning farmers market, especially with the holidays looming. The crafts vendors were sure to have an array of handmade treasures for the season. She and Poppy often took turns going on Saturday mornings because someone had to stay at the inn. With her daughter away and her sister busy with Daisy in the mornings, Ivy and Poppy were managing the weekend guests.

While her niece poured coffee into a large thermos for the dining room, Ivy brought her shopping bags from the pantry.

She turned back to Poppy. "I hate to leave you here alone with this crowd. Have you seen Shelly?"

"I'll be fine. Didn't you see Shelly's text? Daisy had a little accident, so she said she'll meet you there."

Instantly, Ivy was concerned about the youngster. "Anything serious?"

Poppy laughed. "No, Daisy tried to send a little stuffed animal for a swim out to sea, so Shelly had to stop and unplug the toilet. At least she's good at that."

"Not her favorite little seal, I hope?" Most kids liked bears or giraffes, but Daisy had latched onto a seal after she'd seen them on the beach in La Jolla with their baby seal pups.

"Sarah the seal survived, but she might have to take a trip through the washing machine."

Ivy recalled how many times she'd had to rescue stuffed animals or dolls when her daughters were young. "Thank goodness we don't have the plumbing emergencies here like we used to."

Sighing happily, Poppy opened the door to Bertie, one of the vintage twin turquoise refrigerators they'd decided to keep. She reached for the cream. "While I still love this pair of beauties, I never realized I could love modern plumbing so much." Poppy looked back at her and grinned. "Now we can do other things, like digging up vacant lots. Shelly is dying to do that."

"I'll talk to her," Ivy said, smiling as she folded the bags she would take. "I almost miss this old house's quirks. They brought us all together. Remember the first painting party we had?"

The rear screen door slammed, and Bennett stepped inside, wearing his running shorts. He paused to kiss Ivy on the cheek. "That was one party I missed. Tell me again, why I wasn't invited?"

"Because I was trying to put as much distance as I could between me and my old summer crush."

"Best failure ever, sweetheart."

Ivy gave him a playful nudge and kissed him back. "How do you know that wasn't part of my grand plan?"

"Another marriage was the last thing on your mind back then." His eyes crinkled at the corners as he smiled. "Especially to me. I had to work hard on that."

Watching them, Poppy swept her hair to one side and twisted it in thought. "So, how long does it take for the honeymoon to wear off?"

Bennett hugged his wife. "Never, I hope."

"The key is learning to work through our problems while they're small," Ivy said, sensing something behind her niece's question.

Listening, Bennett poured a glass of water and drank it down. "Still in the honeymoon phase with Andrew?"

"I wouldn't put it like that, but he asked me out for dinner this weekend," Poppy replied, her cheeks coloring slightly. "He's visiting and staying with a friend from school who lives here."

"This sounds serious," Bennett said. "Do you think it is?"

Poppy's blush deepened. "I think we're a long way from that phase."

Ivy tucked her arm through her husband's arm. For all his diplomacy in city business, Bennett could be a little clueless about relationships. "Will you walk with me toward the farmers market before your run?"

Now grasping the message, he glanced at Poppy. "Andrew seems like a good guy, that's all."

Ivy steered him toward the door. "Thanks for looking after the inn, Poppy. The coffee is ready, and Room 202 should be checking out soon. See you later."

After they got outside, Bennett spread his hands. "I was just making conversation. What did I say that was so wrong?"

"You know how sensitive Poppy is about dating. Especially after that last fiasco she and Sunny got into with those guys from L.A. She wants to take her relationships slowly now. Asking if every guy she dates is the one only puts pressure on her."

"If she's thinking about it, I don't see the problem. There's slow, and then there's glacial. What I mean is, maybe Mitch and I can help vet guys for her."

"I know you're trying to be helpful, but I wouldn't mention that to her. Women have their ways."

"But the last guy was trouble."

"We should let her forget about that. We've all made

mistakes when we were young. I once met this guitar-playing surfer dude on the beach before I left for university." Ivy slid a side-eyed glance his way. "You know, he never called me like he promised."

Bennett drew a hand over his stubbly jawline. "Okay, point taken. I'll be making up for that for the rest of our lives, won't I?"

"You're off to a good start. I'll let you know how it goes."

"Hold that thought." Bennett stopped to stretch his legs on a stone wall before continuing his run, and Ivy's heart fluttered at the sight of his muscular legs and shoulders. They hadn't been married long, and she still found him wildly attractive.

In fact, even more now than on their wedding day.

She recalled her mother saying that she loved her husband more with each passing year. Ivy hadn't understood it then, because in her first marriage, maintaining a happy relationship with Jeremy had become increasingly difficult over time. She'd been the one putting in most of the effort.

That was before she'd known about his infidelity. When she found out after his death, the knowledge crushed her but had also helped her move on. It had also given her the motivation to rescue and turn the sprawling old beach house he'd bought for another woman into her home and livelihood.

She glanced back at the inn, its new windows and fresh paint gleaming in the autumn sunshine. And just look at it now, she thought, her heart filling with pride at the work they'd all put into the long-overdue renovation.

Bennett caught her glance. "You've done an amazing

job on the inn. I'm so proud of how you persevered. You had a vision, and you didn't let anything stop you."

"I appreciate you saying that. You had a part in it, too."

"We're good together, Ivy."

She slid a hand over his shoulder. "Yes, we are. And I hope you can always feel comfortable sharing troubling issues with each other."

"I thought that went without saying." Bennett nodded toward the beach. "See you later, sweetheart." He paused to kiss her before taking off.

At that moment, Ivy realized she was also holding back.

8

s Ivy approached the farmers market, she heard
Gilda call to her.

She turned to see Gilda pushing Pixie in a dog carrier.
The Chihuahua was reclining on a pink silk pillow and
looking like the little princess she was. Her leg was wrapped
in its splint, but her eyes were bright, and her tail wagged
when she saw Ivy.

"Pixie looks much better," Ivy said.

"Thank goodness for that," Gilda said. "We're on our
way to volunteer at Thrifty Threads. Pixie's splint must stay
on for several weeks, but she's eating normally and seems
happy. Thanks to the fabulous Dr. Caleb."

Ivy nodded, glad that he was there, too. "We were lucky
he knew a little about how to splint a dog's leg."

"Well, he is a veterinarian." Gilda's expression brightened. "He's considering opening a practice in Summer
Beach. I'm surprised you didn't know that."

"We don't investigate guests before they arrive," Ivy

said, smiling. "I assumed he was a medical doctor for humans."

Gilda stroked the dog's head gently. "Dr. Caleb explained that he sometimes consults at that veterinary clinic. He examined Pixie so gently, and had X-rays done before he splinted her leg. She adores him now."

Gilda lowered her voice in a conspiratorial tone. "He told me he's moving from Los Angeles and looking for a fresh start. When I asked him if he had someone special in his life, he told me he'd been seeing an actress, but she's left him. Probably some tart who broke his heart, which means he's available. He might be interested in Sunny or Poppy."

Ivy didn't want to know the details or how Gilda had acquired this information. "While I appreciate you thinking of them, please don't play matchmaker. They're young women, and they can take care of themselves."

Didn't she just have this conversation with Bennett?

Gilda started off for the thrift shop, and Ivy continued to the farmers market. The aromas of apple cider and cinnamon from the bakery stalls filled the air. Near the entry, she spotted a skinny young man at the edge of the farmers market patch, bent over sweeping a pile of vegetable debris into a trash bin. His dark hoodie hung loose on his shoulders as he worked.

Was this the same young man she'd seen near the vacant library lot?

Just then, a child's excited scream erupted behind her, and she turned. Her younger sister hurried toward her with her little girl strapped into a stroller. Both were dressed in sunny yellow sundresses with sweaters looped around their shoulders. Shelly's hair was half tumbling from a messy bun, but the two looked cute together. Smiling, she snapped a quick photo with her phone.

Ivy wore her usual farmers market outfit of jeans and a hoodie. At least they were her good ones.

When Shelly reached Ivy, she scooped Daisy from her stroller. "Here's our sweet bundle of trouble."

The little girl gripped a damp plushie seal in her hand and waved it at Ivy, squealing with glee.

"Got wet," Daisy said in her sweet little baby girl voice.

Shelly quirked a smile. "So we both had to change, and Daisy wanted to dress up."

Ivy laughed at the news and hugged them both. "Glad you were able to fish out Sarah the seal."

"Barely," Shelly said, making a face. "I tugged the stuffed animal out by the tail, but it wasn't easy. I sent it through a super-fast wash cycle and towel dried it. I hope it will air dry in the sun. And here I thought my plumbing days were over."

Ivy put her arm around her younger sister. "Look at you, winning at motherhood."

"Barely." Shelly shuddered. "Can we talk about something else? I'm a little traumatized."

"Let's see what Brooke brought from her garden today." Ivy gestured toward a booth where a table was laden with vegetables.

They greeted the older sister of Ivy's friend, Marina Moore, who had opened a cafe in town. Brooke wore a friendly smile, along with denim overalls and Birkenstock sandals. She tucked wisps of hair into her long braid.

"Why, look who we have here," a gruff voice called out.

Ivy and Shelly turned to see Darla strolling toward

them. Daisy waved her arms and cried out in a sweet sing-song voice to her.

"Mind if I take Daisy for a spin around the market while you shop?" Darla asked.

Daisy squealed with glee, clearly understanding the conversation was about her.

Shelly smiled. "Go ahead, she likes to get out."

With a wink at little Daisy, Darla took control of the stroller. "Come on, kiddo. I feel donuts in your future." She wheeled Daisy away before Shelly could protest.

Ivy laughed while Shelly shook her head. "I have to introduce Darla to fruit and granola."

"One donut won't hurt Daisy," Ivy said. "Lighten up."

Shelly clamped a hand to her forehead. "I can't believe you're throwing my advice back at me."

"Ivy's right." Brooke smiled. "But that's why I started growing vegetables. When my boys were little, they wouldn't touch them, yet they were fascinated when I started growing them. Watching cucumbers and tomatoes grow and eating them off the vine intrigued them. While those aren't technically vegetables, they were close enough for me."

A bushel of small artichokes caught Ivy's attention. "I have to get some of those for Poppy."

"How many?" Brooke asked.

Whatever Poppy didn't want, she and Bennett and Sunny would enjoy, if her daughter was around. When Sunny wasn't working at the inn, she often went out for dinner with friends, even if that only meant grilled hot dogs on the beach or pasta night at a friend's place. Ivy was glad Sunny had made new friends in Summer Beach.

While Brooke helped her select good produce, a woman joined them.

Ivy didn't recognize the younger woman, who wore a cream-colored leather jacket that accented her blond hair. Diamonds sparkled at her ears and neck. While Ivy didn't know everyone in town, she would have remembered this attractive woman. Every item she wore looked expensive.

"What delicate artichokes," the woman said.

"They're so tender, you can eat them whole," Brooke said. "Simply remove the outer leaves and cut the tops. When these are ready to harvest, they sell fast, and I won't have any more for a while." She told her how to prepare them. "Then, serve them with a little olive oil and balsamic vinegar drizzled over them."

"They sound delicious," the woman said. "I wish we could get some, but we've just moved in, and our kitchen is still a disaster."

A tall, good-looking man about Bennett's age joined them. He slid an arm around the woman.

"The Coral Cafe is serving them right now," Brooke continued, her voice rising on a strangled note at the man's arrival. "The chef prepares a lot of seasonal specialties. She's also my sister."

"That must be a new restaurant," the man with her remarked.

Brooke's cheeks flushed. "It's been open for a couple of years." She tried to turn away from the couple.

The woman exclaimed over Brooke's vegetables. "Do you grow everything yourself?"

Noting Brooke's sudden discomfort, Ivy said, "She does. It's all organic and grown on their land."

Shelly glanced at Brooke and the other woman before

asking Ivy, "Do we have any family plans yet for Thanksgiving?"

Ivy hadn't spoken to their brothers yet. "Now that the renovation is finished, we should plan a gathering at the inn for family and friends, and for any guests who might be there."

A slow smile spread across Shelly's face. "Maybe that will include Dr. Caleb. Gilda told me everything."

"Stop that." Ivy nudged her. Shelly knew better than to gossip about guests.

The other woman leaned in, a stack of gold bracelets clinking on her wrists. "I'm sorry to interrupt, but I heard you mention an inn. We need to move out of the house to fumigate. We spoke with the proprietor at the Seal Cove Inn, but she has a wedding party there. It's fully booked. Where is this inn?"

This was a chance to fill some empty rooms. But from the corner of her eye, Ivy saw Brooke shake her head vigorously while rearranging produce.

Shelly caught that, too. She spoke up. "I'm so sorry, but we don't have rooms available. You might check in a neighboring community."

"What a shame, but we'll do that," the woman said.

After the couple moved on, Ivy turned back to Brooke, curious about her reaction. But before she could ask, Shelly picked up a zucchini, wielding it like a microphone.

Shelly leaned toward Brooke. "Care to make a comment about why you warned us against them?"

As shoppers slowed by the booth, Brooke frowned and shook her head again. "I shouldn't say."

Shelly lowered her voice. "Now you *have* to spill the tea. Who was that?"

As Brooke bit her lip and glanced around, an unsettling feeling filled Ivy.

After customers moved away from Brooke's booth, she let out a long sigh. "I didn't know the woman, but I know the man with her. He ran against Bennett in the first mayoral race. All I'm saying is that he fights dirty. I didn't know he'd returned to Summer Beach. And that was not his wife. At least, not the one I knew."

Shelly's eyes widened. "Well, this is uncomfortable. Wish I'd known that."

"Now you do," Brooke said. "There's a lot of history under the sunshine here in Summer Beach. Some of it is unfounded gossip, and some is real."

A sickening feeling gathered in the pit of Ivy's stomach as she watched the couple thread the crowd in the distance. If Bennett knew they'd returned, that might be what was bothering him.

Just then, a little girl carrying a large pumpkin stumbled, sending her armload crashing to the ground.

Immediately, the little girl broke out in tears. "I only wanted to show my mom."

"It's okay, accidents happen here all the time," Brooke said, waving down a teenage boy who was rolling a trash can.

The young girl's mother appeared behind her daughter, promising she'd buy a pumpkin.

"Vanz, could you help clean that up?" Brooke gestured to the pumpkin broken in pieces on the ground.

Shelly touched her arm. "Is that the same guy you saw at the beach?"

Ivy had told Shelly about him. She followed her gaze. "Looks like him. Same hoodie anyway."

Seeing him in the daylight, she remembered seeing him during her beach walks, too. He was always alone, walking with a hunched posture as if he wanted to disappear. She'd seen him that night at the library lot, wearing similar clothes.

"I'm wondering if he might have been the vandal," Ivy murmured.

"Let's find out." Shelly adjusted her bag.

They approached Cookie, who managed the farmers market with the same no-nonsense efficiency she brought to everything in Summer Beach. She stood near her vegetable stand, checking off items on a clipboard.

When Cookie looked up, Ivy greeted and asked, "Who's the boy cleaning up the pumpkins?"

The older woman's weathered face broke into a smile. "That's Vanz. He seems like a good kid. Showed up a week ago asking if anyone needed help. I gave him cleanup duty because he was hanging around looking hungry, and I needed a rest."

"Is he local?" Ivy watched Vanz working diligently, making sure every piece of pumpkin made it into the bin.

"I don't think so. He doesn't say much about himself." Cookie's expression softened. "But he's a hard worker and does what needs doing without complaint. Some of the vendors have been giving him extra fruit and vegetables. He always thanks them and offers to help load their vehicles."

That didn't sound like someone who would vandalize property. Ivy's chest tightened.

"Do you know where he's staying?" Shelly asked.

"No idea. I asked once, but he changed the subject." Cookie glanced toward Vanz, who'd moved on to sweeping the area around the flower stand. "I needed help with clean up and mentioned that to one of the vendors. Vanz over-heard, so he asked what I needed done."

"That was good of you to hire him," Ivy said.

"I give him a little cash for his work, but it's only tempo-rary." Cookie's expression turned thoughtful. "He looks like he has a lot on his young mind. Reminds me a little of Mitch when he first arrived in Summer Beach. Sort of looks like him, too."

Shelly turned toward the teenager. After studying him for a moment, she frowned.

Ivy watched Vanz finish cleaning up the pumpkin and move to straighten a display of squash that had been knocked askew. Not the actions of someone destroying property for the thrill of it.

But she couldn't shake the image of him walking past the library lot that night. He matched the description of what Jen and George's security camera had caught.

Shelly shifted her bag to her other shoulder. "Let's talk to him."

As they approached the boy, he looked up with wary eyes in a lean face. He was younger than Ivy had thought. Maybe sixteen, if that.

"I saw you working," Ivy said. "Cookie says you've been a big help."

"Just cleaning up." His voice was soft, barely audible over the market noise.

"That's important work." Ivy paused, choosing her words carefully. "I run the Seabreeze Inn. If you're inter-ested in more work, sometimes we need help."

Hope flickered in his eyes. "I'm not sure how long I'll be here."

Ivy hesitated. "Are you staying somewhere nearby?"

"I'm fine." The words spilled out, and the boy's hands tightened on the broom handle. "Why do you care?"

"Because people around here look out for each other," Ivy said. "Do you have any family here?"

"Kind of. I mean, I don't know. Not really." His shoulders sagged a little. "I camp out on the beach."

Shelly inclined her head, staring at the young teen and narrowing her eyes, but she said nothing.

Ivy's heart ached at his response. "That must be cold at night."

He shrugged off her comment. "I have a sleeping bag."

"Well, my offer stands," Ivy said. "Come by the inn if you want work. Or if you need anything."

Vanz gave her a quick nod and returned to work.

As Ivy and Shelly walked away, Shelly asked, "What do you think?"

"I'm not sure he's the one who vandalized Java Beach. The timing fits, but he seems like a scared kid who needs help. He should be in school."

Shelly chewed her lip. "I hate to say this, but that kid looks a lot like my husband."

Ivy glanced back at the teen. Sure enough, his profile was similar. "What are you thinking?"

Her sister let out a breath. "One night when Mitch was being brutally honest with me about his past, he told me he'd been pretty wild, and he wouldn't be surprised if there was a knock on our door someday." Shelly sighed again. "Maybe he was preparing me. The age of that kid sort of fits."

Instantly, Ivy realized what Shelly was getting at.

"You think Mitch is his father?"

Shelly's face paled, and she blinked hard. "Why else

would he be hanging around here? Finding out something like that is enough to make even good kids lash out."

"Maybe the likeness is just a coincidence," Ivy said, but Shelly looked convinced. "Are you going to tell Mitch?"

A desperate look filled Shelly's face. "That would change everything. I wish Mom were here. She always knows what to do."

Empathy and compassion surged through Ivy, and she wrapped an arm around her sister. "Me, too, Shells. But I've got you."

9

———

$\mathcal{B}$ennett leaned against the stainless-steel prep counter, watching Mitch flip burgers at Java Beach. The kitchen was filled with the aromas of sizzling beef and caramelized onions, along with the omnipresent smell of coffee.

"Join us on Thanksgiving," Bennett said, continuing their earlier conversation. "Ivy wants to have a big dinner for family and friends at the inn. We've also been talking about having a food drive for those who might not have much of a feast on their tables this year."

Mitch pressed down on a burger, sending up a hiss of steam. "Count me in. I'll help cook. Turkey, sides, whatever you need. As for a food drive, I could ask for donations from some of the local farmers I buy from."

"That would be great. And Shelly already volunteered you to cook." Bennett knew he could count on Mitch.

"Of course she did." Mitch grinned, sliding the burgers onto waiting buns. "It's what I do. Food makes folks happy.

If people could come together over a good meal, I think we could solve all the problems of the world."

"Maybe we'll start here," Bennett said, giving his friend a fist bump.

A soft, tentative knock at the back door interrupted them. Mitch and Bennett exchanged glances.

Bennett knew few people used the kitchen entrance except for deliveries. Those usually came in the morning. A thought occurred to him as Mitch wiped his hands on his apron and opened the door.

The teenager from the marina stood there, hands shoved deep into his pockets. He looked even thinner in the fading afternoon light, his face shadowed by exhaustion.

"Hey," the boy said shyly. "Remember me?"

"Good to see you." Without hesitation, Mitch stepped back, holding the door open. "Come in."

"Smells good in here," the boy said.

Bennett nodded and moved to one side, giving the kid his space.

"You showed up just in time," Mitch said, walking back to the grill. "I'm making burgers, and I have an extra one. Hungry?"

The kid's gaze locked onto the food with an intensity that answered the question. He nodded.

"Good. Give me a minute." Mitch pulled out a fresh patty from the refrigerator and slid it onto the grill. He gave the teen a fist bump. "I'm Mitch, and that's Bennett. What's your name?"

The boy cast a quick glance at them. "People call me Vanz. With a z."

"Cool name." Mitch glanced down at the boy's black-and-white checkerboard slip-on sneakers, now scuffed and dirty. These were popular with kids, especially around the beach. "Because of your Vans?"

A faint flash of pride flickered across the kid's face. "Yeah."

Mitch opened a display case near the door and tossed Vanz a blueberry muffin. "Start with that while I cook."

Vanz snatched the muffin from the air. "Thanks."

"You like avocado burgers?"

"I guess. I've never had one." Vanz ate the muffin in a few big bites.

"Then you're in for a treat." Mitch poured a generous helping of fries into the fryer basket.

Curious to know more about the boy, Bennett pulled out a stool for him. "Are you from around here?"

Vanz shook his head. "Little town up north. You wouldn't know it."

"Try me. I've been around." Mitch flipped the burger, the sizzle filling the silence.

"Palm Vista. Nothing ever happens there."

Mitch raised his eyebrows in surprise. "No kidding? I visited some family there a long time ago. A cousin on my mother's side got married. I don't remember any names, though."

"Wish I could forget it all," Vanz mumbled, absently rubbing a fading bruise on his wrist.

Listening to this exchange, Bennett watched the teenager. As he looked closer, he noticed other bruises and cuts on the boy's hands and neck. He looked as if he'd been in a recent altercation. Bennett wondered if that was with other kids or family members. Then again, maybe he'd fallen on a skateboard or bike.

As Mitch cooked, Vanz relaxed a little, though his thin

shoulders remained tense. He watched while Mitch assembled the burger on a fresh bun with a sizzling patty, sliced avocado, tomato, lettuce, and a drizzle of aioli. He plated it with fries and set it on the small table in the corner where employees took breaks.

"Sit," Mitch said. "Eat your fill."

Vanz stared at the plate for a moment before picking up the burger and wolfing it down like someone who hadn't had a real meal in days.

Bennett continued watching him. This boy was too young to be on his own. He was a long way from home, and he should be in school. He might be a runaway, in which case Bennett should let Clark know to check the missing persons database for a possible match.

He caught Mitch's eye, and the look they shared needed no translation. They both wondered what this kid's story was.

Vanz demolished the burger and most of the fries before slowing down. He sat back, looking almost dazed with satisfaction.

"Looks like that went down easy," Mitch said.

"Yeah." The boy's voice came out rough. "That was really good."

Mitch grabbed a bag from under the counter and loaded it with more muffins and items from the cooler. "You can take this with you."

"You don't need to do that."

"I have to throw them out otherwise. Health department rules." Mitch's tone didn't invite argument. "They're yours. If you come by tomorrow at the same time, I'll probably have something for you. Got to follow the rules."

"Okay, if you have to." Vanz stood slowly, tucking the

bag protectively under his arm. His eyes were fixed on a spot on the floor. "Why are you being nice to me?"

"Why not, dude?" Mitch replied with an easy grin. "You seem like a cool guy."

"Not everyone thinks so."

"Well, we do," Mitch said, glancing at Bennett. "Do your parents know where you are?"

A shadow darkened the teen's face. "They don't care about me."

"That's their loss," Mitch said, tidying his workspace. Lightly, he added, "Got a place to sleep tonight?"

A shy smile tugged at Vanz's lips as he nodded. "I've been camping out. See you later."

With the food clutched against his chest, Vanz slipped outside into the night.

Mitch closed the door and leaned against it, exhaling slowly. "I slipped the address of the local shelter into that bag. Maybe he'll go there."

"It's clear that kid's running from something," Bennett said. "But he should be in school unless his parents gave him permission to drop out. I need to call Clark now so he can contact the Palm Vista police. There might be a missing person report."

"Can that wait until tomorrow?" Mitch turned off the water and reached for a towel. "I'd like to hear his story because he could be in danger if he's sent back." He met Bennett's gaze.

Bennett rubbed his neck. "We have to do the right thing."

"I think we are. Seriously, I've got a weird feeling about this kid. Something's not right at home, and I bet he's safer here. Did you see the bruises on him?"

Bennett heaved a sigh and nodded. "However, that's not for us to decide, even though you might be right."

He recalled how Vanz had tensed when Mitch mentioned Palm Vista. And the kid had eaten that burger like he was starving. For more than food, he suspected.

"I can't help feeling the adults in his life have betrayed him," Mitch said as he cleaned the cooktop. "I'd hate to be another one. That kid needs help, whether he'll admit it to us or not."

"Still, I have an ethical duty to report a situation with a minor," Bennett said, picking up his jacket with a heavy heart.

Although he could understand Mitch's desire to fully understand the issues, once Bennett alerted Clark, as a mandated reporter, the police chief would have to report suspicions of abuse or neglect.

Yet the thought of sending Vanz back to a perilous situation at home was disturbing.

10

*J*vy tapped the number to the police chief's office and asked for Clark. She leaned against the kitchen counter in her apartment unit above the garage at the inn. Shelly and Poppy sat at the kitchen table waiting.

When Clark's voice boomed over the phone, Ivy quickly told him what they were planning. "If anyone asks, we're thinking about a temporary community garden, and Shelly is checking the soil."

A long pause ensued, and Clark finally said, "Ivy, I didn't hear that."

"No, we really are considering that. Depending on how the library and art museum are situated on the lot, we hope to have enough space for a small community garden. Shelly will demonstrate how seeds are planted and show people how to prune and care for vegetables and fruits. It will be part of the learning center."

That last part was a fresh idea, but why not? Ivy thought.

There was another pause. As Ivy held her breath, Shelly crossed her fingers.

"That's different, and it's a commendable plan," Clark finally replied. "You'll let me know if you need any help."

"We will," Ivy promised.

When she hung up the phone, Shelly and Poppy clapped and cheered.

"Operation treasure hunt is underway," Shelly said. "That must be where Amelia hid the gold. Why would she leave all her cash in the bank during a war? If I were her, I'd have something handy in case I had to escape."

"Or it might be more relics she rescued from Europe," Poppy added.

The trio made their way downstairs to the garage and got into Ivy's car. The shovels were still in the trunk. Even though they now had a plausible, and potentially real, cover story, Ivy still hadn't told Bennett or her brother about this.

Because she didn't want to hear a patronizing story about why they shouldn't do this.

Sunny waved to them through the window as they drove off. They wouldn't be gone long, and her youngest daughter had become more reliable than when they'd first arrived.

Maybe Ivy should have let her in on the secret mission, but she'd know soon enough if they found something.

A little later, the trio stood at the edge of the library lot, shovels in hand. Ivy had marked the spot with stones the night they were here last, and now they began digging in earnest, the scrape of metal against earth was the only sound besides their breathing and the distant call of gulls.

"This is exciting," Poppy said, driving her shovel deeper. "As if we're archaeologists."

"Or grave robbers," Shelly added, but her eyes gleamed with anticipation.

A few curious passersby glanced their way, but no one stopped.

After a few minutes, Ivy's shovel hit something solid with a dull metallic sound. "There it is."

"Woo-hoo!" Shelly yelled. "Let's do this."

Ivy knelt in her jeans, brushing away dirt with her gloved hands. The surface beneath looked rough. "Help me clear it."

They worked steadily, widening the hole, searching for the edges to figure out what this was. Ivy's shoulders ached, but she didn't stop. Whatever was down here, she needed to know.

They all did.

They worked together, scraping away soil until a large metal plate emerged. On one side was a recessed handle.

"It looks like a hatch," Poppy said, leaning back on her knees.

Ivy's heart hammered against her ribs. She gripped the handle and pulled. The hatch resisted, sealed under decades of rust and settled earth.

Poppy drew a crowbar from the tool bag she'd brought. "Let's try some leverage."

Shelly let out another enthusiastic cry. "Our niece thinks of everything."

After they took turns loosening the cover, it gave way with a final grinding sound. Together, they lifted the hatch, revealing a pit partially illuminated by sunlight that descended into darkness.

Poppy switched on a flashlight. She swung a beam of

light over the metal ladder rungs bolted to the side of the vertical shaft.

Cooler air rushed up from the opening, carrying the smell of age and damp earth.

Shelly peered over the edge, then immediately stepped back. "Oh, no. No way. I'm not going down there. What if there are snakes?"

"They'd probably be long dead," Poppy said.

"I wonder what this was for." Ivy squinted into the void. The beam caught metal rungs descending into shadow. She couldn't see the bottom.

They all peered down the shaft.

"One of us should check it out," Ivy said.

Poppy nodded. "I can light your way."

Ivy sat back on her heels. "So I guess I'm the one."

Shelly and Poppy looked at each other, grinning sheepishly.

"Aunt Ivy, you're the bravest one, but I'll be right behind you. I can't let you go alone." Poppy attached the flashlight with a lanyard around her neck so she wouldn't lose it. "I have another light with a head mount if you want it."

Ivy slipped the device over her head and tightened. "I feel like a miner."

"Gold miner, I hope." Shelly crossed her arms. "I'll stay up here and be the lookout."

Ivy summoned her courage. "We need to see what's down there."

Shelly shook her head. "Maybe you need to see. I'm happy with mystery and speculation. Just bring back treasure."

Ivy shot her a glance. "As if I'd have anyplace to run off with it. One way in, one way out."

"Shelly can watch for anyone wondering why there's a giant hole in the library lot." Poppy switched to the high beam, sending it sweeping down the shaft. "If someone shows up, tell them we're investigating the water supply."

"Is that what this is?" Shelly asked.

Poppy shrugged. "I have no idea, but who would know any better?"

"All right, here goes." Ivy drew a deep breath and swung her legs over the edge, finding the first rung with her foot. She tested the strength. The metal seemed solid beneath her weight, which was encouraging. She tested the next rung, then the next, descending slowly while Poppy aimed the flashlight from above.

The walls of the shaft were concrete. This wasn't a hastily dug bomb shelter. Someone had taken time and resources to build it.

The Ericksons had the resources, and Amelia had the vision.

The air grew cooler as she descended, and the sounds from above faded, replaced by the echo of her breathing.

At last, Ivy's feet touched solid ground. With her heart pounding, she stepped off the ladder and swung around, illuminating the small space.

She was standing in a room.

"You're not going to believe this," she called out to Poppy above.

This was not a cramped shelter, but an actual underground room about the size of a room in a house. The construction looked old, with a floor and walls made of concrete discolored over the years. Her light beam swept across the space, highlighting items long shielded.

Against one wall was a small desk with a chair. On another stood shelves holding what looked like supplies. A stack of books sat on a table with two chairs.

"Ivy?" Poppy's voice echoed down the shaft. "What do you see?"

"A room. Like a bunker or bomb shelter. It's okay, come down."

After a moment, Poppy appeared on the ladder, descending more quickly than Ivy had. She reached the bottom and immediately raised her flashlight, the stronger beam illuminating more.

"Oh, wow, this stuff is old," Poppy said, pausing her light on several faded magazines. "Have you ever heard of *Life* magazine?"

"That's an old one. What's the date on it?"

Poppy peered closer. "This one's from 1943, and another from 1944."

"And look at all this equipment." Ivy swept her beam over the desk.

Binoculars sat next to what looked like a viewing apparatus. The device looked intricate and specialized, though she had no idea what it was. Several old notebooks with stained covers sat to one side.

"This is incredible," Poppy whispered, moving closer to the desk.

Ivy stood in awe of the dusty treasures. "Remember how Amelia converted the house to care for recuperating service women and men during the war? This must have been a lookout post. The binoculars, the viewing equipment. An attack occurred a little farther north on the coast, so I'll bet this was used to watch for enemy ships. Or possibly as a shelter."

Poppy looked around in amazement. "Maybe both."

Ivy moved to the shelves, finding tins and canned goods with faded labels that were still legible. Other small boxes were wrapped in oilcloth.

Behind them, Shelly's voice echoed down the shaft. "What's taking so long? Did you find the treasure?"

"Nothing like that," Ivy called back. "But something better. A treasure trove of history."

Poppy touched a pin-up poster of a blond woman in a one-piece bathing suit looking over her shoulder. "This is like a time capsule."

"Is it safe down there?" Shelly called out.

"Seems to be," Ivy replied. "The structure is solid. I wish you could see this."

There was a brief moment of silence.

Then Shelly's voice echoed through the shaft. "I'm coming down. But if that ladder collapses on me, I'm haunting both of you forever."

They waited while Shelly descended, complaining about ladders and dark spaces all the way. When she finally reached the bottom, she stood for a moment, breathing hard.

Then she saw the room.

"Oh, my gosh," Shelly said, turning around with wonder in her eyes. "It's like we stepped into a time capsule."

Shelly leaned in for a closer look at the vintage pin-up poster. "That's Betty Grable. I remember her from old films. That's probably worth a small fortune. And those magazines might be worth something. Not gold-level money, but collectors would want them."

Ivy sighed. "Not everything is about money, Shells. Just look at this place. Everything has been well preserved down here. Historians would love to see this."

Ivy picked up one of the notebooks, opening it with care. The pages were brittle and covered in neat handwriting. Dates, times, observations. There were log entries from whoever had manned this post during the war.

"Someone was down here regularly." Ivy glanced through the pages. "They were recording what they saw, so this was an active station."

Then she noticed something that made her smile. At the back of the notebook were doodles and sketches. She looked closer. They were mostly of animals and clusters of fruit, but they were good, like the work of a young, talented artist.

Poppy had moved to a smaller room off to one side. "Aunt Ivy. You need to see this."

Ivy followed her. "There's another room?"

She glanced around. Metal bunk beds stood against one wall.

Poppy swung her light to a corner. "There."

On the other wall was an opening shored up with rough timbers.

"Where do you think that goes?" Poppy asked.

Ivy shrugged. "Maybe that's a getaway passage. Should we check it out?"

Poppy crouched, examining the entrance. "It looks different from the rest of this place. Maybe it was built afterward."

Ivy was about to suggest they explore the tunnel when her light swept across something that made her freeze.

On the lower bunk, hidden in shadows, was a sleeping bag.

Not an old military one from the 1940s. This was a modern roll made of a blue synthetic material, the kind sold at sporting goods stores. And next to it, a dirty backpack and a reusable water bottle.

"Someone's been here," Ivy said quietly. "Recently, I think."

They stared at the sleeping bag, the implications sinking in. Someone had discovered this place, probably via the tunnel.

"We need to go," Shelly said, her voice tight. "Now."

"Agreed." Ivy backed toward the ladder, keeping her light on the tunnel entrance. Was someone down there watching them? Had they heard voices and fled deeper into the passage?

Were they coming back?

Shelly reached the metal rungs first, scrambling up as quickly as she could. Poppy followed close behind.

"I'll be right up," Ivy said.

She brought out her phone and snapped several photos before scaling the rungs. After pulling herself into the bright sunshine, she rested on the ground, catching her breath. Poppy and Shelly looked shaken from their harried exit.

Poppy nodded toward the hatch. "Let's close that."

The three of them eased the creaking cover back into place. They shoveled dirt over it, working quickly to disguise their excavation.

Poppy sat down, breathing hard. "That sleeping bag was new."

"Someone is living down there." Shelly rubbed her arms. "Or hiding. Either way, we just broke into their home."

Ivy recalled something she'd heard. "Didn't Vanz, the teenager at the farmers market, tell us he had a sleeping bag? What if he found this place?"

Shelly shook her head. "This is getting to be too much to take in."

"We should tell someone right away," Poppy said.

Shelly leaned on her shovel. "Tell them what? That we found a World War II bunker with a squatter?"

The implications of their discovery dawned on Ivy. This might slow the development for the library. Or even halt it.

Ivy pulled out her phone but hesitated. If it was Vanz staying there, calling the police might not end well for him. They might never have a chance to help him. She put the phone back in her pocket.

But leaving an underground bunker with someone living in it unsupervised also seemed dangerous. The tunnel might be unstable. If it collapsed while he was inside, he might never be found.

Ivy shuddered at the thought. "We need to bring Bennett and Forrest in on this."

Poppy nodded slowly. "The sleeping bag looked cheap, and the backpack was pretty banged up. Whoever is sleeping down there doesn't have much."

Shelly cast a look at her, and Ivy could tell what she was thinking.

They gathered their shovels and walked to the car.

Ivy glanced over her shoulder. The lot looked like

vacant land waiting for construction, with no sign of the secret beneath.

Poppy opened the car's rear door. "How will we figure out where the entrance to that tunnel is?"

Ivy considered that. "Maybe we'll ask around to see if there are any old tunnels here."

"Then people will wonder why we're asking." Shelly shook her head. "Operation treasure hunt just got a lot more complicated."

"Operation rescue mission," Poppy corrected. "That's what this is now."

As they drove away, Ivy couldn't shake the image of that sleeping bag in the darkness. Someone was hiding in a bunker built to protect people from threats that might have ended decades ago, but not for them.

11

Ivy peered at the computer screen in the library at the inn, scrolling through historical sites about World War II bunkers in Southern California. Others, also hidden for years, had been discovered in nearby Solana Beach and Huntington Beach, the latter known as the Bolsa Chica bunkers. Most were built by the Army Corps of Engineers to scan the horizon for enemy ships, but civilians also built bunkers and shelters.

She suspected that's what the Ericksons had done.

This discovery would be a historian's delight, but there was more to it than that.

Ivy needed to decide today, if she could. Shelly hadn't spoken to Mitch yet, but she'd promised she would.

Ivy remembered the photos she had on her phone. She pulled them up, but the lighting was poor, so she transferred them to her computer to view on a larger screen.

She scanned them, noticing details she hadn't seen before. On the last one of the sleeping bag and backpack, she zoomed in, hoping to see a name tag or some other identifying mark. Instead, she noticed something else.

A paper bag. She zoomed in again to see the printing.

Java Beach.

Ivy passed her hands over her face, then picked up her phone to text Shelly, who was outside planting seasonal flowers in the garden.

Shelly, come inside. I saw something in one of the photos you need to see.

A few minutes later, Shelly appeared in the doorway. "What's up?"

Ivy motioned to the screen. "Look at that."

Shelly sucked in a breath. "Do you think Mitch knows?"

"I think you need to have a serious talk with him."

Shelly sighed. "We need to track down Vanz. I'd never forgive myself if anything happened to him."

"I tried to find him on the beach this morning," Ivy said. "I'm going back out in a little while to search again. And I should talk to Bennett today."

Shelly drew in her lower lip. "Should we do that together?"

"I need to talk to him first. I haven't been completely truthful about what we were doing. If you want us there when you ask Mitch about Vanz, we can be, but we need to find him."

"I think Mitch would want Bennett there for support. If he doesn't know, it's going to be a real shock. And if he does…" Shelly gestured toward the paper bag in the image. "Then we might need a referee. He should have told me."

Ivy nodded at her sister's assessment. "Wait until you hear what he has to say."

The farmers market wasn't open until tomorrow morning, but she would be there as soon as it opened to talk to Vanz. Unless they found him today. She wondered if they should check the bunker tonight.

Just then, Ivy saw Bennett pull his SUV into the car court behind the inn.

"There he is," Shelly said.

Ivy got up to follow Bennett upstairs to their apartment unit above the garage.

"Hi, honey," she called out as she walked inside. "You're home early."

He came in from the bedroom looking distracted, rolling up his shirtsleeves as he walked to the kitchen. "My meeting was canceled. Still, I need to work on something without distraction."

A note in his voice made Ivy pause. "Is everything okay?"

"I have a few things on my mind."

"Want to talk about it?"

"I don't want to trouble you. It doesn't concern you."

Ivy studied her husband. They'd been married long enough that she could read his moods, and right now he was holding something back. But pushing wouldn't help. Bennett would talk when he was ready.

The problem was, she needed to level with him.

"How about I make a pot of coffee? I picked up the season's new pumpkin spice flavor at the farmers market."

"I could sure use a cup."

"I'll bring it outside to you. It's still sunny, and I think the breeze will feel good."

"I'll change first." Bennett went into the bedroom while Ivy made her way to the kitchen.

Grinding beans and setting up the French press gave

her time to organize her thoughts. How would she tell Bennett that she'd gone against his advice, against Forrest's recommendation, and excavated the library lot anyway?

After the coffee brewed, Ivy poured two mugs, put them on a tray with a few cookies, and made her way to their small balcony. They called this their treehouse because the surrounding palm trees created a canopy around the space.

She placed the tray on the table by the sofa and sat down. Moments later, Bennett joined her, having changed into sweatpants and a thick hoodie.

"That smells good," Bennett said, sitting beside her.

The ocean stretched before them, with afternoon sun glinting off the waves like diamonds. Below, the beach was dotted with late-season tourists and locals enjoying the mild weather. Gulls wheeled overhead, their calls rising above the steady rhythm of the tides.

Thinking about how she should start, Ivy cradled her mug. Bennett took the other one, stretching his legs out with a sigh.

"This is nice," he said. "We should do this more often."

"We should." Ivy sipped her coffee, gathering courage. "Darling, I need to tell you something. It's important."

He turned to look at her, and she saw wariness flicker across his face. "Go on."

"Yesterday, Shelly, Poppy, and I went to the library lot." She paused, breathing slowly to calm herself. "We dug up what I'd hit with my shovel during the groundbreaking."

Bennett's expression shifted from surprise to dismay. "You didn't need to do that."

"I know. You told me to wait for Forrest and his crew. Technically, you were right. But I wanted to investigate before heavy equipment destroyed it."

Her words tumbled out now. "I called Clark first and told him we were researching the soil for a potential community garden. Which we're considering, so it wasn't entirely a cover story."

"Why did you call Clark and not me?" His face was lined with hurt and frustration.

"You were at work. And I knew you'd tell me to wait. That wasn't the first time we'd been on the property," she admitted. "Clark caught us there one night."

He furrowed his brow. "What night? Did you sneak out? I don't understand."

"The night we went to the book club meeting. We went there first to investigate, and Clark caught us." Quickly, she told him the entire story. "I'm sorry. I should have told you before we went."

Bennett set down his coffee mug with studied deliberation. "This isn't only about whether you told me first or not. You could have been hurt out there. You should have told me what you were doing."

"I felt outnumbered between you and Forrest, and I was a little hurt that you minimized my concerns. I think we both have a right to be upset, but there's more." She took another breath. "We found something incredible."

He shook his head, but she saw curiosity edging out the frustration, so she faced him and went on.

"Today, we found a hatch in the ground and opened it. We climbed down a chute and discovered a World War II-era bunker. There's a room down there with bunk beds, supplies, and magazines from the 1940s. We also found a lot of equipment, probably for watching the horizon for enemy ships or aircraft. The Ericksons must have had it built as a lookout post or shelter."

Bennett stared at her. "You went down into it?"

"Poppy and I did. Shelly eventually followed, though she wasn't happy about it." Ivy sensed the excitement creeping into her voice, but she couldn't restrain it. "It's like a time capsule. Everything is preserved. I've been researching online and found other bunkers have been discovered in Solana Beach and Huntington Beach. The Army Corps of Engineers built some, while civilians created others for personal use. This fits the Erickson pattern."

Bennett ran a hand through his hair and pitched forward. "Okay, that is fascinating. A genuine World War II bunker on the library property? This changes everything."

"Exactly." Relief surged through her at his change in attitude. "I was thinking we could incorporate it into the library and museum somehow. Preserve it and make it accessible for educational purposes. Imagine school groups being able to see actual wartime infrastructure and read the logs from whoever manned that station."

"There are logs?"

"Notebooks filled with observations. Times, dates, what they saw. It's all there, along with notes I can't make out." She paused, her enthusiasm dimming. "But there's something else we found."

His expression shifted back to concern. "What?"

"We saw a modern sleeping bag on one of the bunks. Someone has been living down there."

Bennett sat forward abruptly. "Living in the bunker?"

"We think so. Everything else was from the 1940s, frozen in time. But we saw new things." She pulled out her phone, showing him the photos she'd taken. "I zoomed in on this one. Look at what's next to the sleeping bag."

Bennett took the phone, squinting at the screen. Then his eyes widened. "Is that a Java Beach bag?"

Ivy's voice dropped. "Shelly thinks that it might be a teenager we saw at the farmers market. Cookie gave some cleanup work to a young teenage boy. He also matches the description from Jen and George's security camera the night Java Beach was vandalized, but I really don't think he did it."

As the palm fronds rustled above them, Bennett laced his hands behind his neck and tipped his head back.

Ivy hesitated but went on. "Shelly has a theory based on what Mitch once told her. She thinks Vanz might be Mitch's son. You haven't seen him, but he looks a lot like Mitch. We're not sure if he knew anything about the boy."

Bennett sat up in shock. "What?"

"She hasn't told Mitch yet, but she's going to. We think Vanz is here looking for his father." Ivy set down her mug, leaning forward. "That would explain why the boy is here."

Bennett stood and crossed to the balcony railing. He gripped it, staring out at the ocean. "I have a confession, too."

Ivy knew something had been bothering him. She sipped her coffee and waited.

"Mitch and I talked to a kid at the marina. He's the same one you met. Mitch invited him to Java Beach because the kid looked hungry. He gave him some food in a bag, so that's probably what you saw in the photo."

"Then you met him, too." Ivy tried not to sound like she was accusing him of withholding information, but she wondered how long he'd known about the boy. "I wish you'd told me about him."

A guilty expression crossed his face. "Maybe I should have."

Ivy let that go. They were talking now, and this was enough. "We think he got in through the tunnel, not the upper hatch. Do you know of any old tunnels nearby?"

"Not offhand, but I can find out."

Ivy stood and joined Bennett at the railing. "We need to find Vanz before he disappears. We suspect he's in trouble."

"I would agree with that."

"Then we'll look together." Bennett turned to face her. "I'm not really upset about you digging up the lot. Exasperated, yes. Worried about you climbing into an old wartime bunker by yourself? Absolutely. But angry? No."

She hadn't expected this from him. "You're not?"

"I admire your tenacity, even when it drives me crazy." He touched her cheek. "You see something that needs investigating, and you do it. You find people who need help, and you help them. That's who you are. I married you knowing that, and I wouldn't change it."

A warm feeling spread through her chest. "Even when I go against your advice?"

"Even then. Though next time, maybe give me a heads up before you descend into underground bunkers?" He managed a slight smile. "Just so I know where to send the search party if you don't come back."

"Deal." She leaned against him, and he wrapped an arm around her shoulders. "So what now?"

"We need to find Vanz," Bennett replied, checking his watch. "We still have a couple of hours of daylight. Then we need to talk to Mitch and figure out how to help a kid who might be his son. If so, Mitch has a responsibility to him. The kid shouldn't live in a bunker because he has nowhere else to go."

Ivy thought about that. "Mitch and Shelly's beach bungalow is small. If needed, we could give him a room here, at least temporarily during the off-season." She didn't mind helping, because soon, Mitch would learn that his life was about to change. He would need the support of family.

Ivy just hoped they found Vanz before he vanished. Or worse.

12

Ivy clutched Bennett's hand, the ocean mist cool on her face. They had left the inn and were walking on the beach where they'd each seen Vanz before, scanning the shoreline for any sign of him. They walked first in one direction toward the cove, then the other toward the village.

Ivy saw a few surfers in the water waiting for the last waves of the day, and other people strolled or walked a dog near the water's edge, but no solitary teenager in a dark hoodie appeared. She'd had such high hopes for finding Vanz. He seemed like a lost kid everyone had turned their backs on.

They could help him, if he'd let them.

"He's not here," she said with a sinking feeling.

Bennett stroked his chin. "If we don't find him, I need to tell Clark. A kid living in an unstable underground bunker isn't safe."

Ivy was torn between wanting to protect Vanz's privacy

and knowing Bennett was right. "But Clark will investigate, and Vanz might disappear if he hasn't already."

"We'd lose any chance of helping him," Bennett added. "This might be Mitch's son we're talking about."

"He could be in the bunker. I still have the shovels and toolbox in the trunk of my car." Ivy told him how they climbed down.

"I hope so," Bennett said. "This discovery is also historically significant for the town. I was unaware of it, although there had been some gossip. Old Charlie mentioned it once a long time ago, but I always thought that was just one of his stories. You know how Charlie is with his coffee cronies at Java Beach, each one topping another with a taller tale."

"Apparently, this one was true." Ivy thought about Charlie, the local small-time bookmaker, and wondered what he knew about this, if anything.

They walked back to the inn and took Ivy's red Chevy convertible that had all their excavation equipment still in the back. Poppy's flashlight and headlamp sat in the toolbox alongside the shovels. Bennett added a coil of rope from the garage.

"Safety precaution," he said. "If those antiquated ladder rungs give out, I want a backup. I wish I had climbing gear, but this will work for now."

"I think it's fairly sturdy." She appreciated Bennett's foresight and caution.

On the vacant lot, Ivy led Bennett to the spot they'd marked, and together they cleared away the camouflage of dirt and leaves they'd scattered over the hatch that morning.

Bennett knelt beside it, running his hands over the metal surface. "This is substantial. Heavy-duty construction." He found the recessed handle and pulled. The hatch lifted with the same protesting groan, revealing the dark shaft below.

Bennett called out into the dim recesses. "Hey, Vanz. Are you down there? We're here to help you. No one wants to hurt you."

They squatted by the edge, waiting, but there was only silence.

"Let's go down," Bennett said.

Ivy illuminated the ladder rungs with her flashlight. "It's solid. We tested it thoroughly."

"Let me go first." Bennett glanced around and secured the rope to a nearby palm tree, then lowered the other end into the shaft. "Just in case a metal rung breaks under my weight. I'm heavier than you are."

He descended carefully, testing each rung before putting his full weight on it. Ivy followed, her flashlight beam dancing across the concrete walls. When they reached the bottom, Bennett stood for a moment, taking in the space.

"This is incredible," he said.

The bunker looked exactly as they'd left it. Bunk beds, desk, supplies, the pin-up poster still curling on the wall. Bennett moved to the desk, picking up one of the *Life* magazines with care.

"May of 1944," he said, reading the cover. "The Allies were planning the invasion of Normandy when this was published. But it would be more than a year before the Pacific conflict ended." He set it down reverently and examined the binoculars and the viewing apparatus. "Given the natural rise of the land, they would have had a clear view of the ocean. This was a real operation. Someone spent serious time here, scanning the ocean.

Likely watching enemy ships on the horizon and then relaying that information."

"Look at the logs." Ivy showed him the notebooks, opening one to reveal the neat handwriting. "Whoever manned this post was meticulous."

Bennett read a few entries, his expression growing more absorbed. "This is town history we never knew. The historical society doesn't have any record of this bunker. Nothing in the official archives."

"Maybe the Ericksons kept it secret." Ivy moved to the shelves, examining the preserved supplies. "It might have also served as a private shelter in case of invasion or attack."

"That makes sense given the era." Bennett looked around the room with new appreciation. "The fear was real. Japanese submarines cruised the California coast, sinking an oil tanker near Cambria and shelling Ellwood oil field near Santa Barbara. A submarine also landed covertly at Point Loma in San Diego. People genuinely believed an invasion was possible."

Bennett took photos with his phone, documenting everything. When he reached the tunnel entrance in the second room, he stopped.

"Where does this go?"

"We saw it but didn't explore. We thought the timbers might be unstable." Ivy joined him, aiming her flashlight into the passage. "Looks like it was dug after the main bunker was built. You can see where the concrete ends and the hand excavation begins."

"Escape route, maybe. Or they were trying to extend the shelter." Bennett crouched, examining the entrance.

"We'd need a structural engineer to assess if it's safe to explore."

"That's for another day. We need to find Vanz." Ivy turned, sweeping her flashlight across the bunks. Her heart dropped. "Oh, no. Everything was right here earlier."

The sleeping bag and backpack were gone. The bunk sat empty, the thin mattress bare except for a wrinkled wool blanket full of dust.

"He must have come back," Bennett said. "Either heard you or saw signs someone had discovered his hiding place."

Ivy's stomach sank. "I hope we haven't driven him away."

"It's possible."

Ivy checked the rest of the space. Nothing else seemed disturbed, except on the concrete floor, she saw a roll of breath mints, the kind Shelly liked. "I'll bet these fell out of Shelly's pocket, and he saw them. He probably grabbed his stuff and took off."

They climbed back up the ladder in silence. At the surface, they lowered the hatch and stood looking at the lot.

"It would be a shame to build on top of this," Bennett said. "To cover it up again when we've just rediscovered a part of the community's history."

"I was thinking the same thing." Ivy brushed dirt from her jeans. "Maybe Forrest could work with the architect to change the plans, or how the building is situated on the land. I thought we might incorporate the bunker into the existing design in some way."

"Great idea," Bennett said, looking at her with admiration. "It would need to be inspected first to assess the structural integrity. But yes, I think it's possible. They might have to adjust the building footprint but having an actual World

War II bunker as part of the library and museum? That's a selling point, not a liability."

"We still need to find Vanz," Ivy said, glancing at the time on her phone.

"We do. And I think it's time to call Clark." Bennett started toward the car. "A teenager living in an unstable bunker is one thing. But a teen who knows we found him and might be desperate enough to make bad decisions is something we need to alert the police about."

Ivy knew he was right, but it still felt like failure. They'd wanted to help Vanz, to reach him before fear drove him away. Now he was gone, and they had no idea where to look.

As they drove back to the inn, Ivy's phone buzzed. A text from Shelly: *Talked to Mitch. He's shaken. Come over as soon as you can.*

Ivy showed the message to Bennett.

"Good, we need to work together to figure out how to find his son, if that's who Vanz really is, before this story ends badly for everyone."

They parked in front of Mitch and Shelly's bungalow as the sun neared the ocean's horizon.

She thought about Vanz, wherever he was now. Running away with a sleeping bag and a backpack, still carrying whatever hardships had driven him to Summer Beach in the first place. Looking for a father who might not even know he existed.

What a tough situation for him, she thought, praying they find him before it was too late.

They just had to find Vanz first.

13

When Ivy and Mitch opened the door to Mitch and Shelly's bungalow, a look of relief washed over her sister's face.

"Vanz just got here," Shelly said. "We have a little emergency."

The teenager sat on the futon looking very small and cradling a kitten in his lap. The small tabby had a bloodied hindquarter, and Shelly knelt beside them with a first aid kit, gently cleansing the wound. Daisy watched from her perch on the armchair, wide-eyed and solemn.

Ivy saw tears in his eyes as he stroked the kitten, comforting it.

"What can I do to help?" Ivy asked.

Shelly looked up. "Could you bring a glass of water for Vanz?"

"I'll help you," Mitch said.

"How are you doing?" Ivy asked when they were in the kitchen.

With a worried look, Mitch ran a hand through his

spiky hair. "This is an awful lot to take in, but I'm going to do the right thing by that kid."

Ivy hugged him. "We're here to help."

"Thanks," he said, reaching into the cabinet for glasses.

Ivy returned to the living room and put the glasses on the surfboard they used as a coffee table. The room had a comfortable beachy vibe, and Vanz seemed to relax a little.

"Do you know what happened to the kitten?" Ivy asked.

"When I was heading out of town, I saw a car hit it," Vanz said without looking up. "One day when I was hanging around Java Beach, I overheard Mitch and Shelly talking about a vet. I didn't know where else to take it. You weren't at Java Beach, so I came here." He paused. "I once followed Mitch home, so I knew where he lived."

The kitten mewed softly, its eyes half-closed.

Ivy pulled out her phone. "I'll call Poppy and see if Dr. Caleb is in or she can reach him."

"Why were you leaving?" Mitch's voice was tight with emotion.

"I did some bad stuff." Vanz kept petting the cat, avoiding looking at anyone. The confession poured out of him now that it had started. "I need to tell you. I sprayed black paint over your mural and threw the chairs around. I was mad at you for not recognizing me when I first came in."

Mitch leaned forward. "Hey, dude, I'm sorry about that. I didn't know."

Vanz looked up sheepishly. "I could've told you. But I was mad at everything when I got here. I took it out on your place, and I'm sorry. I can try to repaint it or work it off."

The boy looked so guilty and miserable that it broke

Ivy's heart. Shelly gripped the first aid kit, preparing herself.

Mitch sat down on the futon near Vanz. "Mind telling me how old you are?"

"Sixteen," Vanz replied.

Rocking slightly, Mitch clasped his hands. "And who is your mother?"

Vanz finally looked up, his eyes red-rimmed. "Her name is Melinda. You probably don't remember her."

Ivy watched the blank look on Mitch's face. She reached for Shelly's hand, squeezing it gently.

Mitch swallowed hard. "I'm sorry, I don't remember."

"My mom and yours are cousins." Vanz's voice cracked slightly.

"Then… then that makes us cousins, too." Mitch ran a hand over his face in relief. "So, why did you come here?"

Vanz stroked the kitten as if he wasn't sure how to answer the question. Finally, he said, "My dad was drunk one night, like he always is, and he blew up at me for not helping him find the TV remote. He locked me out, so that's why I came here looking for you. I had some money saved for a bus ticket."

The words tumbled out faster now, like a dam breaking. "Mom tries to protect me, but he goes after her instead." He shook his head. "She only stays with him because of me. I figured if I left, she'd be free."

Ivy's throat tightened. A boy of sixteen, homeless and alone, trying to protect his mother by running away. "Does she know where you are?"

"She does. Not my dad."

Mitch asked, "Is your mom in danger? Or any brothers or sisters?"

"I'm the only kid," Vanz replied. "But I worry about my mom."

"Oh, sweetheart," Shelly murmured, her eyes bright with tears.

Mitch leaned forward, his elbows on his knees. "You're family. You understand that, right? We're all here for you."

Vanz furrowed his brow, clearly skeptical of this. "But I destroyed your property."

"We can deal with that," Mitch said. "But first, we need to make sure you're safe. And your mom."

Vanz's grip on the kitten tightened slightly, and the little one mewed in protest. He immediately loosened his hold, whispering an apology.

Bennett cleared his throat. "We need to contact the authorities in Palm Vista to make sure your mother is protected, and that she knows you're in safe hands."

"Will I have to go back?" Panic crept into the teen's voice.

"Not to him," Mitch said, setting his jaw. "I'll make sure of that. But Vanz, you're only sixteen. I'll work with your mother to figure out what's best for both of you."

Daisy had been silent throughout, watching from beside Shelly. Now she climbed down and approached Vanz slowly, looking at the kitten.

"Hurt?" she asked in a small voice.

Petting the kitten, Vanz nodded. "He needs a doctor."

"Dr. Caleb could help," Ivy said. "He treats animals."

Just then, Ivy's phone buzzed with a text from Poppy. *Caleb can meet you. I gave him the address.*

Ivy put her arm around Daisy. "In fact, the doctor will be here soon."

Mitch lifted his chin toward Vanz. "We know you were staying in the bunker."

"I didn't touch anything in there." Vanz blinked hard against tears pooling in his eyes.

Shelly touched the boy's shoulder. "You needed shelter. But you can't stay there anymore. It might not be safe."

"So stay with us." Mitch's voice was welcoming. "You can sleep on the futon. Tomorrow, we'll figure out the rest."

They talked more until a knock sounded on the door. It was Dr. Caleb.

Ivy greeted him. "Thanks for coming so quickly."

"Glad you called." Caleb examined the kitten's hind quarter with care. "This little kitten was lucky. Young cats are more resilient."

While Caleb worked on the kitten, Daisy watched in fascination.

Vanz continued petting the kitten. "Dad never let me have a pet. Can I keep him?"

Mitch and Shelly traded a look, and Shelly nodded. "Unless she belongs to someone else, she can stay with you for now."

Seeing Vanz bury his head into the kitten's fur tugged at Ivy's heart.

Caleb was clearly moved by the boy's fondness for the kitten. "Would you mind if I took her overnight for observation? I want to make sure she's okay."

Vanz stroked the kitten and nodded. "You'll take good care of her?"

Caleb squatted to eye level with Vanz. "I promise. And my sidekick, a big furry dog named Starry, loves it when I bring home patients so she can mother them. I have a carrier in my vehicle. I'll get it and come right back for her, okay?"

Vanz nodded with a measure of relief.

Ivy smiled at that, remembering how Starry had looked after Pixie when she was injured. She would ask Caleb if the kitten could stay with him until after they returned from the apple orchard trip they'd planned for tomorrow.

Turning back to Vanz, Shelly asked, "Do you mind if we call your mother?"

Vanz gave her his mother's phone number. Mitch went outside to make the call.

When Mitch returned, he filled Vanz in on the conversation. "Your dad has disappeared, but your mom plans to stay with her sister while she figures out what to do. She asked if you could stay here temporarily. A few weeks, maybe a month or so, until she gets settled."

Shelly smiled at the teenager. "We're happy to have you and the kitten. What will you call it?"

Vanz thought for a moment. "I think she's lucky, so that's what I'll call her. Lucky."

"That's a great name," Shelly said.

When Caleb returned with a carrier, Vanz handed the kitten to him. "Goodbye, Lucky, I'll see you soon."

Caleb picked up the carrier and thanked them all for calling him.

After the veterinarian left, Shelly put her arms around Vanz, and after a moment of stiffness, he melted into her hug. His thin shoulders shook with silent sobs while Shelly held him, and Mitch wrapped his arms around them.

Ivy reached for Bennett, and he clasped her hand, squeezing gently. She watched the heartfelt scene, hoping that Vanz wouldn't flee during the night.

14

The next day, after receiving a call from Mitch, Bennett arrived at Mitch and Shelly's beach bungalow.

Mitch met him outside. "Thanks for coming over. I was relieved to see Vanz still sleeping when I got up this morning. I was afraid he might bolt during the night, but he stayed. He even called his mom this morning. I think he's a good kid at heart. I could be wrong, but I really believe that. His mom seems to have influenced him more than his wacko dad."

"Did you talk to her?"

"Yeah, Shelly did, too. Just to assure her that Vanz was being looked after and not sleeping rough in the wilds of nature. Or in some sketchy area where he might get assaulted. You know how it is. Or maybe you don't."

"Not really, but I can imagine. He's only a kid."

Mitch glanced over his shoulder to check on Vanz through the window. "Did you talk to Clark?"

"I wanted to check with you first."

"It's cool, you can call him now. Come on in. Shelly has a fresh pot of coffee for you, and I made cranberry muffins."

Bennett followed him to the house and greeted Vanz inside. He recognized the kid's fresh T-shirt as one of Mitch's, which was a little large on him. But he'd showered, his jeans were washed, and his canvas sneakers cleaned.

While they spoke, Shelly brought a tray of muffins. He noticed that Vanz took two and ate them hungrily.

He told Vanz that as the mayor, he had to alert Chief Clarkson to let him know of the situation with Vanz and his mother.

When Vanz lowered his eyes and frowned, Bennett quickly added, "Mitch and I will be with you every step of the way to make sure no harm comes to you. You'll be able to stay here."

"I guess that's okay," Vanz said, looking a little relieved.

Bennett went into the kitchen to call Clark. When the chief answered, Bennett quickly filled him in.

"You're with him now?" Clark asked.

"That's right, and Vanz is concerned about his mother's safety. From what he's told us, he has reason to be nervous."

"I'll contact the Palm Vista police department about a safety check for her." Clark paused, listening to Imani, who was with him. "Imani is asking if the boy's mother gave permission for him to stay with Mitch?"

"She did." Bennett could hear Imani in the background giving more advice. Moments later, Clark passed the phone to her to speak.

"Glad you're helping Mitch with this situation," Imani said. "What I was saying is that if Vanz plans to stay here a while, Mitch should have written permission from the mother, appointing him temporary guardian. That way, Vanz can register for school in Summer Beach. I'm happy to help with that."

"That's very generous of you. We'd appreciate that."

Imani added, "If the situation at home is as he says, it's important to keep him out of harm's way or child protective services will have to get involved. But if Mitch steps in to care for Vanz, it will be better for all involved. It's good that he's willing to help."

Bennett recalled when Mitch arrived in Summer Beach years ago. "He went through a tough phase, so he's eager to help Vanz get through this."

"I'd like to meet Vanz. Preferably on neutral ground. May we meet at the inn in a little while?"

"That's a good idea," Bennett replied, and they agreed on a time. He joined the others in the small living room and explained the situation.

"I'm kind of nervous." Vanz rocked slightly on the futon where he'd slept. His sunken eyes loomed large in his thin face.

Mitch put his arm protectively around the boy. "Don't worry, Imani is a friend. She's helped a lot of people get out of bad situations."

Vanz fidgeted with a braided bracelet he wore. "Why help me? She doesn't know me, and I don't have any money. Neither does my mom."

Bennett smiled, trying to put the boy at ease. "Some attorneys will help those who can't afford their fees. They might be paid by the court, or they give their time. That's called *pro bono*, and it's their way of giving back to the community and helping folks who really need it. Imani is part of a legal aid society."

Vanz seemed to consider this. He raised his eyes to Mitch. "Did people help you like this?"

Mitch jerked a thumb toward Bennett. "This guy did. Wouldn't be where I am without him."

Bennett grinned and bumped Mitch's fist. "Mitch was hustling coffee sales on the beach when I met him. He'd developed quite a business with the sunrise surfers, and his coffee was the best around. We wanted him here, and as it turned out, he was worth the bet. Your cousin here is smart and works harder than anyone I know."

Vanz looked between him and Mitch, clearly intrigued by this. "I didn't know how you got started. That's cool."

Bennett realized this might be the first time Vanz had been able to look up to a male relative.

"You could do something like that, too," Mitch said to Vanz. "You seem like a smart guy who isn't afraid to strike out on his own."

Vanz's face brightened. "You really think so?"

Mitch nodded with confidence. "I sure do. I'm good at reading people."

Bennett was proud of Mitch for saying that. Showing faith in a young person could make a real difference in how they perceived themselves and instill aspirations for their future. Mitch had come full circle now.

A little while later, Bennett returned to the inn. Mitch, Shelly, and Vanz followed him. As Vanz entered the Seabreeze Inn, he looked around in awe at the furnishings and the people milling around. Ivy and Poppy were busy tending to guests.

Caleb greeted them in the foyer holding Lucky tenderly in his muscular arms. "Thought you might like to see our little patient. She's doing well, but I'd like to keep her today, if that's all right with you."

Vanz stroked the kitten's head, visibly relaxing. "Sure, that's okay. Thanks for letting me see her."

As Caleb left, Shelly took her little girl's hand. "I'll drop off Daisy with Darla so I can help Ivy and Poppy. Be right back."

"Bye-bye," Daisy said to everyone in a sing-song voice. She kissed her daddy and waved at Vanz.

The teenager looked pleasantly surprised.

Bennett led them to the library where they would have privacy. Mitch and Vanz sat at a table, and Bennett could tell the boy was nervous by his fidgeting.

Presently, Imani swept in, wearing a vibrant pink and orange dress with layers of handcrafted necklaces. Her thick dark braids were arranged like a crown on top of her head, and she carried herself like a queen.

She reached out to shake the boy's hand. "You must be Vanz."

Vanz rose unsteadily and shook her hand.

Mitch gestured for her to sit down. "Imani used to practice in Los Angeles. That means she's seen everything."

"Nothing surprises me, young man." She looked steadily at Vanz. "We can talk privately if you prefer. You won't hurt their feelings. That's called attorney-client privilege. What we talk about can remain between us."

"Can they stay?" Vanz asked.

They all agreed, and Imani began asking questions.

Vanz seemed to relax around her. He answered shyly at first but gained confidence as they spoke.

Finally, Imani spoke to his mother, Melinda. After she hung up, she turned back to Vanz. "It's all arranged. She wants you to stay with Mitch while she figures out a next step for the two of you. She plans to visit as soon as she can. I told her we'd take good care of you while she sorts out the situation with your father."

Relief washed over the boy's face, but then he set his jaw. "I'm not going back as long as my dad is there."

"Do you think he deserves a second chance?"

His face darkened. "He's had a hundred chances. If my mom thinks there's any hope for him, she's wrong. Don't listen to her about him." Vanz began to confide in her, sharing what had happened in the past.

Imani listened carefully before answering. "I understand your point and the issues. Your mother is scared and needs your support, too. I think you'll find she is working on a good plan. Her primary objective is to keep you safe and make sure you return to school."

Mitch added, "We'll take you for some school clothes tomorrow."

Vanz took all this in. "What about my mom? Will she be safe?"

"We'll make sure of it. Chief Clarkson is seeing to that, coordinating with the local police in Palm Vista."

Vanz's shoulders visibly released some of the stress he'd been holding, and he thanked Imani for helping him and his mother.

After Imani left, Bennett turned to Vanz. "As soon as guests are on their way, we plan to go to the apple orchard. If you've never picked apples, you'll be surprised how much fun it is. Plus, there's plenty of apple pie, apple cider, and all the fresh apples you can pick."

Vanz looked slightly confused. "Right off the tree?"

"That's right," Mitch replied. "We'd all planned to go

today, but it wouldn't be the same unless you were there. Best pie you've ever tasted, too."

Vanz hesitated, but the pie angle worked. "That sounds good, I guess."

Bennett rose from the table. "Let's organize everyone. Doesn't take too long to get there. We'll put the extra seat in the back of the SUV. Come help us, Vanz."

As he walked behind Mitch and Vanz, Bennett was struck by how much they looked alike, even the way they walked. No wonder Shelly had thought Vanz might be Mitch's son. Bennett was proud of both how Mitch was handling the situation and the generosity that he and Shelly were extending to Vanz.

This solution was temporary, but depending on what the boy's mother decided, it could turn into a permanent situation. Bennett didn't know if Mitch and Shelly were prepared for that possibility.

15

"What a great idea for a road trip." Ivy turned to Bennett, who was at the wheel winding through the mountains in his SUV.

She breathed in the fresh mountain air, happy that they'd all managed to get away from the inn for a short trip to the nearby Cuyamaca Mountains. Shelly, Mitch, Daisy, and Vanz filled the two back rows of Bennett's SUV.

They'd left Poppy in charge at the inn. Sunny had begged off for plans with friends.

The small town of Julian was known for its apples and apple pies, and this weekend was their annual harvest event, a tradition that dated back more than a century.

Ivy glanced back at Vanz, who pressed his fingers against the window, eyes wide with wonder. Since coming to stay with Mitch and Shelly, he'd started to relax. His shoulders were less hunched, and a shy smile crossed his face from time to time. But this was the first time she'd seen him look guardedly excited.

"Those trees don't look real." Sitting in the last row,

Vanz pointed at a cluster of trees, their leaves turned golden yellow in the autumn sun. "What are they?"

"California black oak trees," Shelly replied from the middle row. "The leaves are losing their chlorophyll, which causes them to turn yellow. Wait until we get higher up on the mountain. It gets even more impressive."

"I've never seen leaves change colors before." Vanz's voice held amazement. "In Palm Vista, leaves go from green to dead."

"That's because Palm Vista is in the high desert." Shelly twisted in her seat as she spoke. "Here in the mountains, we get four real seasons."

"Trees, trees." Daisy bounced gleefully in her car seat between Shelly and Mitch, pointing out the window.

Shelly had dressed Daisy in an apple-red dress with a blue denim jacket and cowboy boots. She wanted to take photos of her daughter today.

"All these trees are amazing." Vanz's voice held a sense of awe that Ivy found endearing.

She caught Shelly's eye and sensed they were both wondering what kind of life he'd known. Clearly, this was quite a departure from his usual life.

Bennett navigated a hairpin turn, and a new vista opened before them. Mountains rose around them, with a valley visible far below.

Vanz caught his breath. "It's so beautiful."

Ivy's throat tightened with compassion. This runaway boy who'd been existing in an underground bunker and had been so angry and lost that he'd vandalized property, needed to see this kind of natural beauty that soothed the soul.

"Look at that." Vanz pointed again. "Are those cows?"

In the distance, Ivy saw a small herd of brown and white cattle grazing in a meadow.

Bennett grinned at the question. "Those are Holstein dairy cows. A lot of small farms up here have livestock."

The boy's eyes lit up. "Can we stop and see them?"

"We'll have plenty of animals to see at the orchard," Bennett said. "They usually have a petting zoo with goats and chickens. Maybe some pigs."

"Pigs, pigs," Daisy echoed, clapping her hands.

Something caught Bennett's attention, and he slowed, pulling into a turn out off the road. "I saw a deer. Let's watch for a minute and see if she comes out again."

A hush came over them as a doe emerged from the trees, her burnished-red fur sleek in the sunlight. Vanz sat still, watching the deer with an expression of pure wonder. The animal paused, ears swiveling, then gracefully bounded away into a stand of trees.

"That was amazing," Vanz whispered.

Bennett pulled back onto the road, climbing higher. They wound past maple trees with leaves turned burnt orange and Sierra gooseberry trees aflame in a blaze of crimson. Wild turkeys decked in brown and gold feathers strutted and pecked in a meadow, their heads bobbing for grubworms.

They crested a rise, and Julian came into view, spreading before them. The small mountain town was lined with wooden storefronts preserved from another era. As they passed a cider mill and a pioneer museum, Vanz and Daisy took it all in with a sense of wonder.

Ivy called out, "Who wants apple cider? The nonalcoholic type, of course."

"Speak for yourself," Shelly said with a wink.

Bennett chuckled and parked by a cider mill that advertised fresh apple cider on a faded sign. When they piled out of the vehicle, crisp air stung Ivy's cheeks. She zipped up her fleece jacket. While it was still sunny, the breeze was brisk. They'd all worn jeans, sweaters, and lightweight jackets.

They warmed themselves with hot cider and splurged on cinnamon-spiced apple pie. Ivy watched Vanz, whose mood had lifted. He seemed to be adapting and enjoying the journey.

Feeling full, they returned to the SUV to continue through town toward Volcan Valley, just a few minutes outside of town.

As they neared the apple orchard, Bennett pulled into the parking area. Families wandered through rows of apple trees, carrying paper bags. The air was sweet with the scent of fresh apples, and goats bleated nearby.

"I see red apples," Daisy exclaimed, spying the trees.

They climbed out of the SUV, and Vanz turned slowly to take it all in. "This is like another world."

Mitch purchased some bags and handed one to Vanz. "I love the beach, but it's pretty cool up here. And so close. Ready to pick some apples?"

Vanz took the bag, a small smile tugging at his lips.

Shelly lifted Daisy from her car seat, and the toddler immediately reached for Vanz.

He looked uncertain, but Mitch nodded encouragingly. Vanz let Daisy hold onto his hand as they walked slowly toward the orchard entrance.

Daisy babbled happily, identifying things with her new words. "Look, birds, trees, apples."

Mitch and Bennett followed behind them, watching them.

Ivy fell into step beside Shelly.

Her sister nodded toward Vanz, biting her lip. "Do you think he's going to be okay?"

"I think so," Ivy replied. "He'll probably need someone to talk to about what he's been through. Maybe a school counselor. But this is the best chance in life he's ever had."

Shelly smiled at that. "I didn't think I'd be ready for a teenager yet, but he seems like a sweet kid. Mitch has really stepped up for him. That makes me love my husband even more."

Ivy sensed that Shelly was mentally preparing herself. "You're going to be okay, too. Come on, let's catch up with them and make some memories."

They jogged ahead to join the others. Soon they were armed with bags and began plucking ripe red Empire apples from the trees. Their sweet fragrance smelled delicious.

Ivy laughed as Shelly hoisted Daisy to pick apples.

"Hold it right there," Mitch said, snapping a photo.

The toddler stretched her little hand toward a red apple, tore it from the tree, and dropped it into their bag. She turned her face up to Shelly. "More, Mommy. More."

Shelly blew stray strands of hair from her face and glanced at Mitch. "Are you still taking photos? I can't hold her much longer."

"I'll take her now." Mitch switched places with Shelly.

Quickly, Ivy took her phone from her pocket to take pictures. She caught all three of them laughing. This day reminded her of how she used to take Misty and Sunny apple picking when they were young.

Daisy shrieked with delight as her father hoisted her onto his shoulders. Her tiny fingers clutched fistfuls of his sun-bleached hair. Suddenly, she yanked it, and Mitch yelped, dropping the bag of apples slung over his shoulder. Shelly leapt over the apples rolling all around them.

Ivy laughed as she snapped a series of photos. "Got it."

Looking over her shoulder, Bennett laughed. "That's a great shot. Look at their expressions."

Mitch made a face. "You want to trade places?"

Bennett shook his head. "My hair is too short for her to hang onto."

Vanz quickly knelt to help pick up apples.

Knowing how much this outing meant to her sister, Ivy kept taking photos. In a few months, snow would blanket this quaint mountain village that was so close to Summer Beach.

Ivy filmed a short video, recalling how she used to take her daughters to play in the snow in Boston as kids. But she and Shelly had grown up along the sunny Southern California coast.

Ivy turned to Shelly. "Remember when Mom and Dad used to bring us up here to see the snow?"

Shelly's eyes brightened. "We'll have to do that later this year. Daisy can build a snowman, and I'll teach her how to throw snowballs at Daddy."

Daisy laughed and squealed at the idea.

Shelly motioned to Ivy and Bennett. "Come help us. Before Daisy gets cranky, we need more apples for all those pies Mitch has planned."

"She's doing fine," Mitch said. "Ginger Delavie gave me some family recipes for apple pie, apple fritters, and an almond-apple butter cake. Those will go well with our pumpkin spice coffee."

"Sounds like you'll be busy in the kitchen," Ivy said.

"Anything for my girls." Mitch grinned as he plucked an apple for Daisy, and Shelly kissed him on the cheek.

Laughing, Ivy snapped a few more photos. She noticed Vanz holding back, so she encouraged him to join them. He was a little awkward at first, but Mitch clowned around with him until he laughed.

"Look at Daisy go." Shelly picked an apple with her daughter and laughed, placing it in the canvas bag slung across her shoulder. Already half-full, the bag bounced against her hip as she reached for another branch. They switched off with Daisy again.

A few minutes later, Mitch emerged from between the rows, his paper bag bulging. Leaves clung to his flannel shirt. "This is so cool. Maybe we could invest in an orchard up here someday."

"Don't even joke about that," Shelly shot back, though her smile softened the words.

Ivy watched her sister's easy banter with Mitch and Vanz as they picked apples. Mitch instinctively steadied Shelly when she stood on her toes to reach higher fruit, and Vanz shyly helped her pick apples.

Bennett held out his hand to her. "Let's pick some apples, sweetheart."

"We need a lot of apple pies for our extended family." She tucked her hand into his. "We'll have a huge celebration this year."

Ivy's mind was spinning with Thanksgiving feast possibilities. Pumpkins arranged across the inn's wide front terrace, strings of lights giving a soft glow, and a buffet laden with a harvest-themed menu.

Bennett chuckled. "We should fill a barrel with water and have apple bobbing. The kids would love that."

"More, Daddy." Daisy's high voice rang out. She was perched on Mitch's shoulders, reaching toward an apple just beyond her grasp.

He obliged, lifting her higher.

After they finished picking apples, they loaded them into the back of the vehicle. Next, they stopped for pumpkin soup at a cafe and then stopped to buy pies.

"Can't go wrong when a place is called Mom's." Mitch took his time to choose the best-looking flaky pies to bring home with them. "We'll have homemade pies for our big feast, though."

As the pies were being wrapped for take-out, Daisy began to grow tired and fussy.

"Babe, can you hurry?" Shelly held Daisy in her arms, pacing to soothe her. "I think we need to get back on the road. Daisy is growing tired. I hope the car ride will lull her to sleep before she starts screaming."

Mitch was paying for the pies. "Just a minute."

"She's had a big day." Shelly bounced Daisy to quiet her cranky cries.

Vanz watched with interest as they hurried back to the vehicle to put Daisy in her car seat.

When they all got back into the SUV, Daisy was irritable from exhaustion, so Bennett started the engine right away. But the low rumble agitated her even more. She let out an ear-piercing scream.

"That was impressive," Mitch said, trying to distract her, but it wasn't working.

"Wow, Daisy-cakes." Shelly tried to give her a bottle, but Daisy pushed it away. "You're hitting the high opera notes now."

Ivy had been through this before, but it was clearly new to Vanz. He put his hands over his ears, his eyes wide at this new development. He picked up one of Daisy's toys, but the red-faced child just pushed it angrily away.

"She doesn't mean that. She's overtired." Shelly put her hand on Bennett's seat. "Just get on the road, and please hurry."

Bennett put the vehicle in gear and eased back onto the road. Sure enough, within a few minutes, the rhythm of the vehicle on the twisty road calmed Daisy, and she began to suck on her bottle, satisfied at last. Her half-lidded eyes finally closed, and she nodded off.

Relieved, Shelly drew a hand across her brow. "Thanks, guys. I know that was a little tense. But she always falls asleep in the car. You have no idea how many times we've driven the coast road to soothe her so we could get some rest."

Ivy turned back to her. "That's how I used to get Misty to sleep when all else failed."

"And to think I missed most of that fun," Bennett said, smiling. "I experienced a little of that with my nephew Logan, but he was a pretty good kid, at least when I was around."

They all settled into their seats for the ride back to Summer Beach. Ivy's mind wandered as she thought about the holidays ahead and how they would pull off a harvest feast for the entire family.

She wanted this year to be special, particularly for Vanz. As soon as they got home, she would start making a list.

At the top of her list would be a call to Forrest to discuss the underground bunker and the impact that would have on the library and museum. At the very least, the structure would have to be inspected and probably reinforced. Shelly's community garden might be out of the question now.

She hoped they could still build over the bunker, because she didn't want to remove this piece of history.

All that would cost more than they'd budgeted.

Then, another thought struck Ivy. She would have to inform Lea, Amelia's great-niece from Germany who funded this project, about the potential cost overruns given this new discovery. She couldn't ask Lea for more money.

Suddenly, the viability of the project seemed bleak.

16

*I*vy strolled through the garden with Shelly in their gardening boots. "This will be a busy week with the cooking school guests coming in."

They'd trimmed back or cleared out the early tomato plants that had run their seasonal course.

Ivy was helping because Shelly had been devoting time to Vanz in the last couple of weeks, making him comfortable in their house, registering him for school, and buying him new clothes. His mother said she would visit soon, but Ivy wondered if the woman was just saying that or if she meant it. Still, Vanz was settling into a routine, and his mental health was improving. Imani had been so thoughtful and gracious in helping him.

As the two sisters worked, they discussed ideas for seasonal garden changes and decorations for the inn, from pumpkins to poinsettias.

Shelly removed her gardening gloves after clearing the last of the spent plants. "How about we set up a spooky Halloween house in the bunker, call it a dungeon of horrors, and charge admission? That would help pay for preservation."

Ivy was skeptical, and she couldn't tell if her sister was serious or joking. With Shelly, you never quite knew.

Although the thought was amusing, Ivy said, "I don't think it's safe, and it would destroy the integrity of the bunker as it is now."

"Oh, my gosh, you thought I was serious?" Shelly mussed Ivy's hair and laughed.

Ivy smoothed her hair back. "You're incorrigible. I wish Mom and Dad could see how little you've changed."

Shelly's expression fell, and her lower lip trembled. "I can't believe you said that. I really try, and you know how much I look up to you."

Instantly, Ivy realized she'd hurt Shelly's feelings. "Hey, I didn't mean it. Look at all you're doing for Vanz. I'm so impressed."

"Ha, ha, got you again." Shelly chuckled.

Ivy shook her head, but this was part of Shelly's kooky charm. "Like I said, incorrigible. But I had a thought about the bunker. It's a real time capsule, so I thought about making a time capsule for Summer Beach residents. They could put meaningful items or writings in it, with a promise to open it at some point in the future. What would you put in it?"

"My best heirloom seeds and Mitch's recipes. What about you?"

"Good question," Ivy said thoughtfully. "I'd have to think about that." How could one distill a complex, richly lived life into a few trinkets to share wisdom or meaning?

They were still trying to ascertain Amelia's motivations for her actions. Every time they learned one thing about her, another chapter opened. Ivy had the feeling there was still so much more to discover about the woman and her life.

Those were thoughts for another day, or a languid evening in front of the fireplace.

She and Shelly climbed the front steps of the inn and paused on the wide terrace.

"Picture this," Shelly began, spreading her hands like a director as she spoke. "Autumn-themed wreaths on the door and windows. We can use them through the end of the year by changing the decorations from fall harvest to Christmas. Less cost, less storage, and a fun project for Sunny. Maybe Vanz would like to pitch in. I'll show them how, and video it for my social channel to bring people in."

"I like that idea," Ivy said. "What about Halloween decorations? This is a major stop for trick-or-treaters. We don't want to terrorize the youngsters, but they'd like a little spooky fun."

"We could fashion ghosts from our white bedsheets by tying them over balloons, then illuminate them with special lighting. We can have an entire family of apparitions." With a glimmer in her eyes, she added, "Maybe our Amelia spirit will join in the fun."

Ivy frowned and held a finger up to her sister. "The jokes are over. Don't go there. If you start that rumor, even during Halloween, it might never die down."

Shelly laughed. "Oh, my gosh. Chill, Ives. I'm only kidding."

Although Ivy sensed the presence of the former owner, she wouldn't admit to Shelly how often or how real those feelings had become. Ivy had been terrified people might believe the inn was haunted and not patronize it, especially a few years ago when she desperately needed the business to work after Jeremy died.

But now?

She shivered. To face that was to agree with everything her sister joked about, and she wasn't quite ready for all of Shelly's woo-woo shenanigans.

Ivy put her hands on her hips. "Do you talk like that to annoy me or because you really believe all that ghostly stuff?"

With a playful whack on Ivy's arm, Shelly laughed again. "Who cares? Where's your sense of fun, Ives?"

"I'm serious, have you ever actually had an encounter in the house, or has all this conjecture been for fun?" Now Ivy really wanted to know.

"What do you think?" Shelly waggled her eyes and flounced into the house as gracefully as she could in overalls and garden boots, where Poppy was looking after Daisy.

"Take off your boots," Ivy called after her, shaking her head. Would her sister ever grow up?

Then, an uncomfortable thought seized Ivy.

Why would she ever want Shelly to change?

Her younger sister brought the fun and levity to life, whereas Ivy worried too much about responsibilities, financials, and how things looked to others. Worrying never solved anything; only planning and action.

While she and Shelly somehow balanced each other, she was the one in danger of growing old in mind and spirit before her time.

Her sister, infuriating as she could be, had a valid point. This season, Ivy resolved, she would lighten up her worries.

And yes, she would invite Amelia, she thought with a nod. Maybe Amelia would sit in that kitchen chair that sometimes gave Ivy the creeps to watch Diya Donnelly at work in their kitchen.

She smiled at the thought.

Diya was a chef and cookbook author known for her spicy fusion cuisine, combining traditional Indian spices with Italian, French, and other cuisines. Her books and public broadcasting television show were gaining in popularity, and her social media followers were climbing.

Although they'd only had a few weeks to plan it, Diya was thrilled to host an autumn-themed cooking school at the inn. Ivy worked out a deal with her for a percentage of the room rates for the attendees she brought. The chef was pleased with the arrangement and eager to escape a snowstorm in Vermont for a sunny week at the beach, even in the slightly cooler off-season.

The cooking week guests would arrive soon.

Ivy heard a car in front of the house, and she turned to see her brother Forrest parking in front. He waved and walked up the palm tree-lined path.

"What a surprise," Ivy said, greeting him.

"I had a consultation here and it ended early, so I thought I'd have lunch with Bennett. We got fish tacos from Rosa's food truck, then went to see that bunker. Bennett took me through it. I hope you have some time to talk about it."

"Sure, let's go inside." She took off her gardening boots by the door and carried them inside toward the kitchen.

Bennett found the bunker so intriguing, he had been taking people down to see it. Mitch, Sunny, and even Boz from the planning department. Darla had peered down the chute, though she wouldn't climb down into it.

While her brother talked about his impressions of the

bunker, Ivy put her boots outside the rear kitchen door and changed into low-heeled boots. They moved to the kitchen table and Forrest reached for a chair.

"No, take that one," Ivy said, pointing to another.

"What's wrong with this one?"

"It's been…unsteady." She smiled and sat down. "What do you think we can do about the bunker? I'd like to preserve it."

Forrest laced his fingers. "I think we can if we moved the main structure closer to the front of the property. However, you'd need a variance from the city to do that."

"Boz might be favorably inclined." At least, she hoped he would be.

"We'll also need to have the existing structure examined and make reinforcements as needed." He paused. "Do you know anything more about it, other than what's there?"

"I contacted local and state historians to inspect it. We know the Ericksons were hypervigilant about protecting art, culture, and people from harm during the war. The bunker was probably a private effort, but it might have been part of the protection efforts here on the West Coast. A team of history professors, graduate students, and other experts are piecing together a probable story based on historical facts and timelines. We hope to learn more soon."

"A civilian effort?" Forrest shook his head. "I don't know. The construction looks like the work of the army's engineer team that built others on the coast during that time. I could be wrong, though. And you need to have that tunnel checked out. That was a clear addition, likely by a private party constructed either at the time or later."

"We haven't found anything that would indicate people had been down there after the war. The magazines, the canned food, the logs, they all date from the end of the war. Nothing later."

Forrest nodded. "I imagine no one wanted to go down there after the war ended. They had lives to get back to."

"Assuming we're able to shore up the bunker, I don't know if we would allow the public in or limit entry to researchers and historians."

"We have a lot to figure out before that," Forrest said. "There's much more down there than initially meets the eye."

Ivy wasn't sure what he meant about that, but she understood a decision on the bunker would come later if they could work around it.

"We had another idea," Ivy said, shifting the conversation. "What about a community garden on the back part of the lot?"

"That's an interesting idea. How much land do you want to dedicate to that?"

"Think of this as the starter project."

"Sounds like an idea of Shelly's."

Ivy leaned forward and put her palms on the table. "She'd like to teach people how to grow food they can eat, ranging from kids to retirees. It would be for people who want a hobby or those whose budget is constrained."

"It's a good idea," Forrest said, clearly considering it. "Shelly knows what she's doing. Her horticulture training isn't wasted. She's done wonders with the nearly dead landscaping that was here when you guys arrived."

Ivy recalled what a mess the grounds were in. "A lot of what we serve here comes from her gardening efforts."

"I'll get the right people out to inspect the structural

integrity and survey the lot again. I'll have to readjust the estimate."

"Do you have any idea of extra costs?"

"Not until we know what we're dealing with. I'll be as kind as possible, but I must pay my workers."

"I understand. And you should have a profit. Lea Martin would insist."

Forrest only shrugged. "When this project is finished, we'll gain plenty of work from it."

"Do you have plans for Thanksgiving yet?" Ivy thought her brother's wife might welcome the invitation. "We're planning a feast here, and you're all invited."

"That's a big invitation for all of us," Forrest said. "Angela will be relieved, so please count us in, thanks. We're expecting Coral and Summer to come home for the holiday."

"I heard. Poppy is excited to see her sisters."

"Rocky and Reed might eat twice their weight, so we'll bring whatever you need."

Ivy chuckled. His twin boys were hard workers. Rocky spent many days at sea working in research, while Reed burned up energy in construction.

He swung out from the table. "I have to check on Reed's job site, but I'll be in touch."

Ivy showed him out, thinking about the extra work ahead to preserve the bunker. She was convinced it would be worth it from a historical perspective, but it wouldn't be without challenges ahead.

Shelly sauntered into the kitchen. "A guest stopped me, asking questions about the gardens. How's Forrest?"

"Working on figuring out the project."

Poppy pushed open the door behind them. "Mom just texted me with a turkey and happy faces."

"Wow, word travels fast." Ivy laughed. "Everyone is coming for Thanksgiving. Family, friends, and guests are welcome."

"We have a couple that booked a holiday here from Italy," Poppy said. "I don't think they know what kind of holiday Thanksgiving is. Can we call it the Harvest Feast of Thanksgiving?"

"That has a nice ring to it," Ivy replied. "I'll ask Diya to help us plan a menu." She loved the idea of entertaining a lot of people, even though a few weeks later, they would have their annual Christmas and holiday open house for the community.

But first, they had to prepare for Halloween.

Just when she thought she'd have a chance to relax after the high summer season, the fall was turning out to be nearly as busy.

17

Ivy balanced a tray of freshly baked pumpkin shortbread and chocolate chip cookies as she nudged the kitchen door open with her foot. "Does everyone have their costumes ready?"

Sweet aromas followed her into the grand foyer where Bennett was untangling string lights.

Her husband looked up, stole a shortbread bar, and winked at her. "I'm still not convinced a mayor should dress up as a pirate."

"It's Halloween. Even mayors get to dress up." She set the tray on the entryway table and straightened the orange and black runner. "Besides, you look dangerously handsome with an eye patch." She kissed him for emphasis.

"Hmm, maybe I will change," Bennett said playfully. "I love your pirate wife outfit."

She wore a flouncy skirt with a blousy top and large hoop earrings. She'd blacked out a couple of teeth and applied red lipstick.

The doorbell chimed, echoing through the foyer.

"Our first trick-or-treaters already?" Bennett checked his watch. "It's barely twilight."

"The little ones start early."

Ivy picked up the bowl of individually wrapped cookies, each nestled in a cellophane bag tied with a Seabreeze Inn ribbon so parents would know where they came from. "Sunny spent all afternoon on these, and we need to finish packaging the rest."

She opened the door to find three small wide-eyed children dressed as a purple dinosaur, a butterfly with colorful wings, and a tiny firefighter with a red hat. They giggled at Shelly's makeshift ghosts, but they were uncertain what to do with their trick-or-treat bags.

Their mother stood behind them, showing them how to hold out their bags and whispering the words they'd forgotten in their excitement.

"Trick or treat," they finally yelled.

"What wonderful costumes you have." Ivy dropped a cookie package into each bag. "These are homemade cookies from the Seabreeze Inn."

The mother thanked them. Emboldened, the kids turned toward the neighboring house, where Darla was dressed as a witch with a black pointed hat. She waited on her front porch, seated beside a steaming cauldron and flickering pumpkins.

Halloween was one of Darla's favorite holidays because she loved dressing up. Every year, she spent the entire day in costume, going to Java Beach with her friends and buying candy.

As the children scampered away, Shelly appeared at her side, dressed as an apple tree, complete with leaves and apples hanging from her costume bark. She placed a thermos of hot cider on the table next to a stack of paper cups.

"Mitch and I finished setting up the ballroom. We made a spot for the DJ and his equipment."

"Perfect." Ivy saw Vanz walking through the hall toward them, dressed in ghoulish black. The transformation in him over the past weeks was remarkable. His posture showed more confidence, and his eyes met hers without immediately darting away.

"You look great, Vanz," she said. "Want to help with the trick-or-treaters?"

"Sure." He seemed happy to have an important job to do.

The doorbell chimed again. "You're on. Here are the cookies. Offer the adults a cup of hot cider from that thermos. Help yourself to the cookies we haven't wrapped yet."

The doorbell rang again. And again. Within half an hour, a steady stream of costumed children flowed onto the porch. Ivy spied princesses and superheroes, ghosts and witches, and an elaborate octopus that required parental assistance to navigate the front steps.

From the kitchen doorway, Sunny called out, "A fresh batch is ready. Sounds like we need more at this rate."

"Told you so," Shelly replied, packaging the cooled cookies.

Inside the ballroom, guests were arriving for the private party. A couple had booked every room for a Halloween party when their travel plans fell through.

Dr. Caleb had met them at breakfast, where they'd talked about their horses and Maltese puppies, so they'd invited him to the party.

Caleb arrived downstairs dressed in his real scrubs with

a stethoscope around his neck and a plastic snake draped over his shoulder.

"Some might call your costume cheating," Ivy teased as she passed through with empty platters.

His eyes crinkled as he smiled. "Maybe a little, but I prefer to think of it as authentic."

Caleb stopped to help Mitch hang fake cobwebs before going to the party.

"He looks pretty good in scrubs," Shelly whispered. "Who do we know for him?"

"If you're thinking of Sunny, she already told me he's not her type. And Poppy has been talking to Andrew, Viola's nephew and attorney."

"No kidding?" Shelly brightened at the gossip.

"Don't mention it to her. You know how she wants to keep her dating life private after those guys from L.A. that she and Sunny dated."

"What jerks they were. Caleb seems like one of the good ones, though. Seems a shame to let him go to waste."

Ivy laughed. "I doubt that he is. But he's also focused on establishing a practice here and finding a place to live."

Shelly inclined her head. "Why here, I wonder?"

"He told me his parents used to come here on holidays, and he loved it. He said he's tired of big cities and the L.A. scene. Evidently, a woman broke his heart."

"An age-old story. Her loss, someone else's gain."

They were all having a good time, and the doorbell's chime became nearly continuous as dusk settled. The trickle of trick-or-treaters quickly became a flood. Families were making a visit to the historic inn part of their Halloween tradition.

Vanz held up a nearly empty bowl. "We're almost out of cookies."

"We have more." Ivy ducked into the kitchen where Poppy and Sunny were laughing as they took out another batch from the oven.

Gilda burst through the back door, her pink hair tipped with green and styled in wild spikes. She held Pixie in her arms and wore a lab coat splattered with what looked distressingly like blood but was probably food coloring.

"Mad scientist?" Ivy asked.

"Mad veterinary technician. Inspired by our handsome new vet. Pixie's costume matches his." Pixie wore tiny scrubs that she wasn't terribly happy about.

"The DJ is setting up," Bennett announced, poking his head into the kitchen. He'd changed into his pirate costume. The eye patch and jaunty tricorn hat were spot on. "Mitch has the popcorn machine going now."

As darkness fell, the trick-or-treating reached its zenith before gradually subsiding.

Shelly appeared with a tray of glasses shimmering with pink liquid. "I thought some of you might like a Sea Breeze cocktail. Fully loaded on the right, and virgin versions to the left."

"You're a lifesaver," Ivy said, taking an icy glass. Tart cranberry and grapefruit combined with vodka hit the spot.

Meanwhile, the ballroom party was in full swing. The DJ had brought an impressive collection of vinyl. He was spinning "Monster Mash," "Ghostbusters," and Michael Jackson's "Thriller" as costumed guests danced.

After a while, Ivy retreated to the patio for a few moments of calm. She admired the fairy lights twinkling overhead. She saw Bennett walking toward her.

As the music shifted to a slower beat, he held out his hand. "Do you dare to dance with this old pirate?"

"Not so old, I think," she replied, stepping into his embrace.

They swayed beneath the soft lights to the sound of the music and the ocean beyond. Over Bennett's shoulder, Ivy saw Mitch teaching Vanz a new card trick. Shelly held Daisy's hands as the little girl toddled around in a bumblebee costume.

"What are you thinking?" Bennett asked, following her gaze.

"That the inn feels so wonderfully full of life." She rested her head against his firm shoulder. "And that I need Diya's help in menu planning. The guest list keeps growing."

"We'll figure it out," he said, his breath warm against her neck. "We always do."

18

"It's amazing that we're completely booked up again with this cooking week," Ivy said to Poppy, closing the drawer where they kept keys at the front desk. The last-minute Halloween party had turned last week into a success. "You and Diya are a marketing dream team."

Poppy smiled at the compliment. "She's a lot of fun to work with. And everyone loves yummy food. Are you and Shelly still visiting the pumpkin patch today?"

"After the cooking school is in session," Ivy replied. They were adding more for the fall harvest feast, and Shelly wanted to take photos of Daisy in the pumpkin patch.

Having checked in the last guest for the start of their cooking week, Ivy and Poppy sat down at the front desk to catch their breaths. The inn was full of guests hungry for Diya Donnelly's autumn specialties. The plan was for them to cook during the day, preparing an evening meal. They would dine in the formal dining room or create a casual setting on the patio under the stars and heat lamps, with an ocean serenade in the background.

At least, that's how Diya described it. She would also show them how to decorate their tables with ordinary objects elevated with flair, from rustic to elegant. She planned to adorn driftwood with pine branches and arrange multicolored gourds around them.

Their high-spirited high priestess of the kitchen had swept in with her supplies like a whirlwind.

"Should we check on Diya?" Poppy asked.

"I think we should."

They made their way to the kitchen, where Diya had commandeered the area in her chef's whites, her long, dark auburn hair pulled back at the nape of her neck. As she barked orders, an assistant scurried around to fulfill Diya's vision.

"Darlings," Diya said, opening her arms to them. "How about a hot cup of cranberry tea and my chai sugar cookies?"

Ivy smiled at the other woman's enthusiasm. "How can we resist?"

They perched on the stools at the long center island, which was ideal for cooking instruction, giving students space to work in the industrial-sized kitchen built for large-scale entertaining and catering teams. Even though this house had been the Ericksons' summer home, they lived a life nearly as grand here as in San Francisco.

That thought reminded Ivy that she should call Viola, the current owner of the Ericksons' main residence, who helped raise funds for the inn's renovation with a grand gala last year. Viola and her niece Meredith would be intrigued at their most recent discovery.

Over tea and cookies, Ivy asked Diya about a harvest feast menu.

The chef whipped out a small spiral notepad and pen. "I have some fabulous ideas for you. That is, if that handsome husband of Shelly's is cooking."

"We couldn't do it without him," Ivy said.

Diya nodded her approval. "He's talented and understands food, so this menu should be easy enough for him to create. With helpers, of course. He'll need a sous chef."

"He'll have plenty. Bennett usually handles the grill with him."

"Oh yes, I remember your dear mayor." Diya sipped her tea, the steam curling around her animated face. "Now, about this harvest feast of yours. I have some ideas to make your guests forget every boring turkey dinner they've ever suffered through."

Ivy wrapped her hands around the warm mug. "I'm intrigued. But we do have some traditionalists on the guest list."

"Trust me." Diya leaned forward, gesturing with her hands as she spoke. "We'll anchor the dinner with turkey transformed. Imagine the meat marinated in yogurt with garam masala, slow-roasted and glazed with pomegranate molasses."

Poppy's eyebrows lifted. "That sounds delicious."

"It's just the beginning." Diya tapped her fingers on the countertop. "Instead of the usual mashed potatoes, you can have a roasted butternut squash puree with brown butter and sage, topped with crispy fried curry leaves."

That sounded fabulous to Ivy, but she knew some would miss the mashed potatoes. Maybe they could prepare both.

"Now for other side dishes," Diya said, making notes. "I

recommend charred brussels sprouts with mustard seeds and coconut, sweet potato chaat with tamarind chutney, and a wild rice pilaf with dried fruits and pistachios."

Ivy glanced at Poppy, a silent message passing between them. The menu sounded exquisite but far beyond what they'd planned.

Diya paused, noting their expressions. "Too much?"

"It sounds amazing," Ivy said. "I'd love to make those recipes sometime. But for the big feast, I'm thinking of one of my brothers who considers ketchup the perfect condiment."

Diya made a face but added, "Classic dishes with subtle twists work well for the less adventurous. How about an herb-roasted turkey with a twist of star anise in the gravy? Garlic mashed potatoes with brown butter, and carrots glazed with local honey and a touch of cardamom." She crossed off some items and added others.

Poppy nodded. "That might work better."

"And for the pescatarians, you can add a seafood option," Diya said. "Sea bass or tilapia in a coconut milk sauce with saffron. Or make an Italian cioppino with a touch of ginger and coriander."

"Fancy," Poppy said. "I love those dishes."

Ivy was suddenly hungry, but she thought of her brother. "Maybe something less fancy?"

Diya handed Ivy the menu ideas. "Since we're in California, grilled fish tacos are an acceptable seafood alternative—just don't let anyone put ketchup on them. That would be a crime against all that I stand for."

"Fortunately, my brother speaks fluent salsa." As Ivy thanked her, the kitchen door swung open, and the student guests began to arrive.

Caleb was among the group. Ivy introduced him. "Dr. Montana is one of our guests who signed up for your class this week."

Diya's attention shifted. "Excellent. Both medicine and cooking require precision."

"Veterinarian, actually. I hope my attention to detail carries into your domain. And call me Caleb."

Diya smiled at him. "Anyone who cares for animals has my admiration."

Others joined them, including a retired couple from Seattle, a young woman with a food blog, and a middle-aged man who confessed that he was a widower learning to cook for himself.

Diya clapped her hands for attention. "It's time for everyone to select a station so we can begin. You'll find an apron that is yours to keep, along with ingredients and instruction for the dish you'll make for our dinner. Let's begin, shall we?"

Ivy caught Caleb's eye as he frowned at the recipe instructions at his station. He threw up his hands, looking a little amused and embarrassed. "I'm clearly diving into the deep end."

Ivy chuckled, but it was time to leave them all to it. She touched Poppy's arm, and they slipped through the kitchen door, closing it against the rising chatter behind them.

"What about that menu Diya suggested?" Poppy asked.

"I'll put Mitch and Diya together. Whatever comes out of that is up to Mitch. Sometimes the best way to handle decisions is to get out of the middle and let those who know what they're doing decide."

"How large is the guest list now?" Poppy asked as they walked back to the foyer.

Ivy ticked off names on her fingers. "Your family and Flint's are coming, along with Shelly and Mitch, plus Bennett's sister and her family. Let's include Gilda and Darla, of course. I hope Vanz's mother will come, and then there's Jen and George. Jen has a sister, Jessica, whose husband shipped out for another tour in the Navy. They have three children, and I hate for them to be alone. Jen and Jessica also make the most wonderful French pastries from old family recipes."

"I remember. Those are delicious." Poppy did a quick count in her head. "That's about thirty-five people so far, Aunt Ivy. Probably more. I know you love to invite friends." She took out a pad of paper from the front desk. "I'll create a guest list and shopping list to make sure we have enough food. Anyone else you can think of?"

"There might be a few more," Ivy said as Poppy started her list. "I wish Mom and Dad could be here, but they're visiting friends in South Africa. After that, they'll have a long voyage crossing the South Atlantic to Brazil with a stop in St. Helena."

Poppy tapped her pencil. "My dream is to be like them someday. Sailing around the world in their seventies is amazing."

"We all want to be like them." Ivy imagined the adventures they were having along the way, and she was truly happy for them. They were living their best life, but she still missed them.

"Bennett and I will provide the main dishes and most of the side dishes unless people want to pitch in," Ivy said. "People will bring desserts, so that will help."

"I love the variety," Poppy said. "It's smart that you added those additional electric ovens during the renovation for events and cooking school weeks. They will come in handy for the holidays."

"I thought we'd use the ballroom this year and serve buffet style," Ivy said. "We have plenty of warming units we can plug in. With all the chandeliers lit, it will be beautiful."

Ivy had been looking forward to hosting everyone in the newly restored space. With the new electrical system, she didn't have to worry about tripping breakers anymore. That was a luxury to her.

Even though they would have a lot of family and friends joining them for the harvest feast, the house would handle them all this year.

Poppy made her list. "So it seems the only thing we have to worry about is having enough food for everyone's taste."

"So it would seem," Ivy said, smiling. "But let's not jinx it." As she'd come to learn, anything could happen with a crowd that size.

19

"We're here at the pumpkin patch," Ivy said, lowering her sunglasses to glance back at Daisy, who clapped with glee.

Bennett pulled into a parking area delineated by square bales of hay. Here, just an hour inland from the cooler coastline, the sun still slanted its warmth across harvested fields, transforming them into an autumn wonderland.

Daisy broke free the moment Mitch unbuckled her from the car seat.

"I want pumpkins." She pointed toward the patch filled with pumpkins of every color.

"You can choose one you want, sweetie." Shelly caught her before she could dart in front of cars. "Remember, we hold hands here."

Ivy took in the scene spread before them. The Riverside farm had transformed its pumpkin patch into a storybook event. Scarecrows with flannel shirts and floppy hats guarded the area, their faces painted with broad grins.

"Look at that giant one." Bennett pointed to a display

near the entrance where a massive pumpkin rested, surrounded by smaller gourds in shades of orange, creamy white, and mottled green. Even fancy striped pumpkins.

"That huge one wouldn't fit in our vehicle," Ivy said. "I bet it would take a forklift to move it. I had no idea they could grow that large."

Mitch hoisted Daisy onto his shoulders. She gripped his hair with her fingers, craning her neck to see everything at once. Shelly had chosen an orange knit set for Daisy's first pumpkin patch photos.

They joined the stream of families moving through the entrance. A teenager offered them a wooden wagon with high sides and squeaky wheels.

"For your pumpkins," the girl said. "We also have a hot coffee and cocoa stand with homemade churros."

"Thanks, that sounds good," Mitch said, taking the handle.

People were taking photos beside a vintage red 1940s farm truck filled with pumpkins. Children darted around bales of hay stacked into mazes and forts while parents trailed behind with wagons and cameras.

Daisy wiggled with excitement on Mitch's shoulders.

He lowered her carefully, keeping hold of her hand. She immediately pulled toward a squat orange pumpkin with a crooked stem.

"I want this one, Mommy!"

"We just got here, baby," Shelly said. "Let's look at a few more first."

But Daisy had already wrapped both arms around it. The pumpkin was nearly as big as she was. She tried to pick it up but fell back and rolled over. She sat up, giggling with hay in her hair.

Ivy pulled out her phone to take photos. "That's a cute shot."

The light was excellent, so she snapped more pictures of Daisy straining against the pumpkin, Mitch helping her, and Shelly having a hearty laugh.

Bennett wandered ahead, examining pumpkins and sorting them.

When Daisy saw him doing that, she looked intrigued. She cast aside the first pumpkin and ran after him.

Shelly held up her hands. "What did I just tell her?"

Ivy laughed, but she loved how serious and discriminating Daisy and Bennett looked. *Snap. Snap.* "Are you grading them on excellence?"

"We're being thorough." Bennett stood, brushing dirt from his jeans. "This is important. Not just any old pumpkin will do, because I know you. You want unusual, original ones you can use for artistic inspiration."

She blew him a kiss and snapped another photo.

Daisy continued to trail Bennett, with Shelly and Mitch in close pursuit. They ambled through the pumpkin patch, with Daisy stopping every so often to pat a new pumpkin. Some she declared too big, others too small, another too bumpy. Her babbling commentary was a sweet soundtrack.

Ivy fell into step beside Shelly while Mitch and Bennett debated the merits of traditional orange versus more exotic varieties.

"She knows what she likes," Ivy said, watching Daisy reject another perfectly good pumpkin.

"As we all do. It's incredible how observant they are at this age. We watch what we say now because she's a little copycat." Shelly adjusted the straw hat she'd worn against the sun.

Moments later, Daisy's shriek of delight got their attention. She'd found one she wanted, a medium-sized pumpkin with perfect symmetry and a curled stem. She sat beside it in the dirt, stroking it like it was a pet.

"This one," Daisy said.

They walked over to inspect the selection. Mitch was listening to Daisy babble on about the pumpkin.

"That's a good one," Ivy said, crouching beside her niece. "Very round."

"Round," Daisy echoed.

"That's right," Ivy said, repeating the word. Her niece's vocabulary was expanding. Shelly and Mitch took turns reading to her every night.

Bennett approached with several pumpkins in a rainbow of colors on a flatbed cart. Orange, white, and green striped pumpkins.

"I love the assortment," Ivy said.

After purchasing, they loaded their selections into the wagon. Daisy insisted on walking beside her chosen pumpkin to ensure its safety. The wagon wheels protested the weight as Mitch pulled it toward the farm stand.

The stand was a permanent structure, weathered wood painted barn red. Its awning provided shade, and beneath it stood long tables displaying jars of honey, apple butter, and preserves with handwritten labels. A chalkboard advertised the drink menu: *Hot Apple Cider, Hot Cocoa, Fresh Churros.*

The aromas hit them first. Cinnamon, cocoa, and baked goods.

They ordered five hot cocoas and several churros. The woman running the stand had kind eyes and an apron dusted with cinnamon. She poured from an industrial dispenser, topping each cup with a swirl of whipped cream.

They found a spot at a picnic table under a massive oak tree, its leaves just starting to turn yellow at the edges.

Ivy sipped her hot cocoa. It was rich and thick, made the old-fashioned way.

Daisy got more whipped cream on her nose than in her mouth. Shelly matched her, and Daisy giggled hysterically about it.

"You two are so silly. And I love it." Ivy bit into a warm churro, twisted and dusted with cinnamon and sugar.

"Heavenly," Shelly said, swooning. Daisy climbed into Mitch's lap, chocolate-smeared and content, examining a tiny gourd she'd somehow acquired.

Mitch whispered something that made Shelly laugh, and her cheeks flushed.

Bennett pressed his knee against Ivy's beneath the table. "There's still love there."

"Here, too." Ivy took another sip of cocoa, feeling its warmth spread without quite reaching the small knot beneath her ribs. She planned to call Misty later. Just a casual check-in. Nothing weird, like Shelly said.

Though knowing herself, she'd probably make it at least a little weird.

Bennett spoke low enough that only she could hear. "You got quiet. Are you okay?"

"Just thinking."

"About?"

She glanced at Shelly, who was trying to stop Daisy from waving her churro like a magic wand. The little girl was tapping it to fling sparkly sugar all around them.

Ivy smiled at that. "Daughters. And the things they don't tell their mothers. Misty in particular."

"She loves you," he said. "That part doesn't change."

Ivy knew that. She did. But loving someone and telling them everything weren't the same thing. Maybe that was a lesson she still needed to learn with her daughters. How to let them go and not expect them to tell you everything.

Unless they wanted to, she told herself, crossing her fingers behind her cup of cocoa.

20

Ivy stood in the entryway of the inn with her hands on her hips, surveying three large bins overflowing with canned goods and boxed items.

Sunny had volunteered to run the project. The hand-written sign she'd taped above the bins, "Holiday Food Drive," had generated more response than she'd anticipated.

Mentally calculating how many families they might feed with the bounty, Ivy turned to Sunny. "The response was good. These are nearly full."

"Mom, you have no idea."

"What do you mean by that?"

"Follow me."

With her strawberry blond hair streaming past her shoulders, Sunny led her to the storage room and opened the door. "What do you think?"

"Oh, my goodness." Ivy was astounded at the effort Sunny had put out.

Boxes of food stood in stacks against the wall. Bags of

rice, pasta, canned vegetables, and even some toiletries and gently worn jackets and sweaters filled the boxes. This was far beyond what she'd imagined they might collect.

"This is truly amazing. We'll need to make two trips to deliver everything. How did you manage all of this?"

"I put up posters around town. But what really brought in the donations was the car wash. One bag of food for a free wash, and another bag for an interior vacuum."

"Where did you do this?"

Sunny grinned. "When you were away at the pumpkin patch. I told you I had plans. I didn't know how much we'd do, so I wanted to surprise you. A couple of friends and I talked a car wash into giving us an hour before they opened. The owner was so impressed, he donated money for us to buy turkeys. We also got all our friends to clean out their parents' pantries."

Sunny looked so pleased with her efforts that Ivy threw her arms around her daughter. "You far exceeded my expectations."

Sunny laughed. "For a change, right?"

"Not at all. I've always been proud of you and your potential."

A knowing expression filled Sunny's face. "I just hid it well for a long time."

Ivy shrugged that off. "Let's just say you were evolving."

"Well, it took a while." Sunny quirked a grin, much like Shelly's. "Now I feel bad about that first-class ticket home from Europe I put on your Amex Card before I came back. That was bratty of me, but I had no concept of the price of things back then. Now I realize how much that must have hurt you financially."

Ivy had to admit that. "It was exasperating at the time."

"I was hurt because Dad died, and I guess I wanted to hurt you for that. I don't know why I felt that way, but I thought if you'd taken better care of him, he'd still be around. And he never denied me anything like you did."

"Oh, sweetheart, I'm so sorry you felt that way." Her husband had died suddenly of an aneurysm that had given no warning.

"It wasn't rational. I know that now." Sunny waved a hand at the donations. "Maybe this is me trying to make up for it. I'm not perfect, but now I realize that. I used to think working at the inn would be easy, but it's not. Guests expect a lot, and they're not always reasonable. Like that sorority reunion where they all jumped into the pool, naked and drunk."

Chuckling, Ivy shook her head. "We can laugh about that now. I was just thankful that woman didn't die on us." She had hit her head, nearly drowned, and Ivy had brought her to safety. It wasn't the woman's finest moment.

Sunny crossed her arms. "Except they posted it on social media. Now we get calls asking if we still allow nude parties at the pool. I thought those were prank calls until someone mentioned the sorority and the posts. This is a tough business, Mom. I had no idea."

Ivy was glad her once-spoiled younger daughter was starting to appreciate her efforts. "Let's start loading the SUV. I'll get the dolly from the garage."

Half an hour later, Bennett emerged from the shower after his morning run. He wore jeans and a faded Summer Beach Volunteer Fire Department sweatshirt. A matching baseball cap shaded his eyes.

Bennett eyed the stacks of boxes and baskets Ivy and

Sunny had assembled by the SUV. Sunny was lifting them in.

"I see the Seabreeze Inn guests have been generous," he said.

"This was all Sunny." Ivy told him the story. As she did, she saw Sunny's modest smile.

It took them nearly an hour to load the SUV, with Bennett carefully arranging and rearranging to make everything fit, but they'd still need to make two trips.

"That should be the last of it," Ivy said, handing Sunny the last bag of pasta.

Every available space was filled in the vehicle, except for the driver's seat and one passenger seat.

Ivy eyed the remaining boxes. "Let's put the rest in my car. Sunny, do you want to drive it?"

Her daughter's eyes brightened at the chance to drive the vintage, cherry-red '57 Chevy convertible. "Sure. That's such a cool car. Can I put the top down and turn on the heater?"

"Whatever you like." Ivy had never let her drive it before because of Sunny's irresponsibility. But now, her daughter seemed like she could handle it.

They loaded the large trunk and the wide back seat and placed an armful of jackets in the front.

With Sunny following, Bennett maneuvered the SUV through town. Ivy watched the familiar scenery pass by. Boutiques and restaurants on Main Street were putting up decorations, and people were wrapping palm tree trunks with lights.

"The village will be lit up tonight," Bennett said.

Ivy loved this time of year. "It feels like the holidays are really on their way now. I wish this spirit of generosity could last all year."

"Then it wouldn't seem special."

She gazed at the sparkling decorations going up in shop windows. "But how lovely life would be."

"I can't disagree with that."

As she thought about this, she realized this was the feeling she tried to capture in her paintings. A sea could be stormy and rough or sunny and smooth. Life wasn't without its challenges, but her job as an artist, as she saw it, was to share sunny skies and the feeling that a beautiful day at the beach might evoke.

She placed a hand on Bennett's arm. "Have I told you how much I appreciate you doing this with us? Not every husband would spend his Saturday delivering food donations."

"That's because not every man has a wife with vision." He took her hand and kissed it.

This, she thought. This was a loving partnership. How fortunate she was to have found it.

They stopped at the school first, where volunteers helped them unload items for the annual turkey giveaway for families who needed help. Ivy loved seeing how excited the children were and the gratitude in the parents' faces.

Ivy understood how much it meant to them to be able to provide for their families. Most people endured hardships at some point in their lives, whether financial or health crises, or something else. Being part of a small community like Summer Beach meant that, unlike the anonymity of a large city, such hardships usually didn't go unnoticed.

Teachers observed a lot, which is why they'd organized this event years ago and continued it to this day. Ivy saw

Celia and Tyler, Bennett's former neighbors from the ridgetop who'd found success in technology before retiring at an early age. Celia had adopted the school music program to aid it, and Tyler was now helping and expanding their assistance.

Celia waved, and Ivy chatted with her for a few minutes. Several teachers also thanked them as they left.

Next, Bennett pulled up to the shelter building a few blocks inland. She saw Shelly's Jeep in the parking lot. The old vehicle had been passed through all the kids in the family and was still running. Mitch was already parked in front, and Sunny parked behind them.

Mitch got out of his vehicle. "Look who finally made it."

He walked toward them. His sleeves were rolled up to his elbows. "The frozen turkeys are unloaded, so I can give you a hand. After this, I need to head back to Java Beach for the lunch run."

Inside, the community shelter buzzed with activity. Behind the dining room and the main activity rooms, volunteers sorted donations into categories. Canned goods, dry goods, personal hygiene items, clothes, and baby supplies. Shelly stood at a table with Daisy playing beside her in a makeshift play area, checking items off a list as they came in. Vanz was helping people select the items they needed.

"About time you showed up," Shelly said when she spotted Ivy and Bennett. "Daisy was starting to think Aunt Ivy had forgotten about us."

"Never," Ivy said, bending down to give her niece a quick hug. "We just had more donations than expected, thanks to Sunny."

Bennett, Mitch, and Sunny began to carry in boxes. The director of the center and other volunteers thanked them as they brought in items. Once the cars were emptied, they stayed to help sort donations.

While doing this, Ivy noticed Bennett and Vanz helping a young mother with two small children select items to replace what they'd lost in a fire. Their manner put the anxious woman at ease.

Across the room, Mitch was demonstrating to an older man how to operate a can opener with his one remaining good hand. Both were laughing at some shared joke.

"Bennett is good with people," Shelly remarked, appearing beside Ivy with a clipboard.

Ivy nodded toward Mitch. "So is your husband."

"We both got lucky."

Ivy thought about the people for whom this center was a lifeline. "Luck can be elusive for some. Here one day and gone the next. It's nice to have a community that cares."

As they worked to unload and sort the donations, Ivy noticed an older woman in a far corner of the room. She was well dressed but sat alone, watching the activity with tired eyes.

Daisy toddled between tables, helping by moving items from one pile to another, while Shelly and Mitch pretended not to notice the disorganization in her wake.

Ivy finished her work and went to get a cup of coffee from the volunteer station. She saw the slender, silver-haired woman in the corner look at her with interest, so Ivy poured a second cup and approached her. Something about the woman was intriguing. Maybe it was the way she'd coordinated her colorful clothing and accessories.

Ivy offered a cup. "Would you like some coffee?"

Surprise crossed the woman's face. "Why, yes. Thank you, dear."

"I'm Ivy," she said, taking a seat beside the woman.

"Adelina," she replied. "I've heard about you. You're the mayor's wife and you run the inn. I've heard it's quite lovely."

"We work hard to maintain it," Ivy said. "How long have you been coming here?"

The woman's fingers tightened around the coffee cup. "I arrived last week. I lived in a neighboring community, and I never thought I'd end up in a place like this at my age. I don't feel old or elderly, but that's how society sees me."

Ivy listened as Adelina shared some of her story. She lived on a fixed income now that couldn't keep pace with rising rents. After her husband's passing, she was left with half the retirement income and a mountain of confusing medical bills. She'd landed here, too embarrassed to call the only distant relative she had.

"I could still work if I had a chance," Adelina said. "Some people here can't."

The familiar narrative broke Ivy's heart, especially coming from someone who reminded her so much of her mother.

"We're glad you're here," Ivy said after listening to her story. "I understand the city is working on some housing assistance programs. Would you be interested?"

Adelina's eyes brightened slightly. "I would. There must be a waiting list though."

"I'll see what I can find out for you."

"If only I could continue working."

"What do you do?"

Adelina sighed. "I'm an artist."

Ivy's interest was piqued. "Would you tell me about your work?"

A wistful smile lifted the corners of her mouth. "I'm a glassblower and mosaicist, meaning I design and create mosaics. At one time, I had a waiting list of clients. But during my husband's extended illness, I lost first my will to create, and then my studio. I thought I could pick it up again, but that chapter is closed now. Still, I miss creating beautiful art."

"I love mosaics. Did you ever create anything in the style of Gaudí?"

Adelina pressed a hand to her heart. "When I was young, I spent time in Barcelona, so Gaudí and the Catalan modernist movement inspired me. Of course, La Sagrada Família and Parc Güell touched my heart. Gaudí's whimsicality and vibrancy have always made me smile."

"I imagine your art has brought smiles to many faces, too."

Ivy recalled the beautiful grape-laden light fixture that Emilie had showed her. In speaking with her, she'd learned that Emilie wanted more items but had been unable to find the artist again. This woman might know of them.

"How did you learn glassblowing?"

"From my father. He learned the original methods in Italy. As a young man, he came here during the war and enlisted in the military. However, he was injured and sent to recuperate in Summer Beach at Las Brisas del Mar. Do you know about that phase of your inn's history?"

"I do," Ivy replied. They spoke about that for a few minutes.

"My father wasn't one to sit still, even though he wasn't

well enough to return to active duty. He once told me how he continued to aid the effort by watching for enemy ships along the coast. Most people don't remember or know anything about that."

Ivy felt a prickle on her neck. "Did he ever mention a bunker?"

"Why, yes." Her eyes widened. "It's probably been built over by now. How do you know about that?"

She wasn't sure how much to say. "There is a group of historians and researchers I'd like to put you in touch with. They're investigating right now. Would you mind?"

"I'd love to share what I remember."

Ivy promised to put her in touch and took her name. Soon, she realized, she should make an announcement to the community, but not until they could secure the entrance against intruders.

They worked through the afternoon, sorting, organizing, and helping visitors select what they needed. Not everything went smoothly. Ivy accidentally knocked over an entire carton of stuffing, and Bennett opened a bottle of soda that stained his sweatshirt and sprayed everyone nearby, but the mishaps only made them laugh more.

As the afternoon wound down and the stream of visitors slowed, Ivy found Bennett in the storage room, organizing the last of the donations.

"Helping here meant a lot to me," she said, leaning against the doorframe.

"To us and everyone, I think. Though next time, I'll be more careful opening sodas."

"Where's the fun in that?" Ivy teased.

With his sweatshirt now bearing stains, Bennett pulled her into a hug, but she didn't care.

With their work done, they prepared to leave.

"Ready to go?" Bennett asked.

"In just a moment." A thought crossed Ivy's mind. She wanted to speak to Adelina again. About several things, in fact.

Adelina had called what she'd seen in Barcelona *whimsical*.

That's what Ivy wanted for the library art museum. Could Adelina create mosaics that would capture the joy she and many others had discovered in Summer Beach?

Ivy thought she could. Art that would beckon to more treasures within.

The idea excited her.

Furthermore, she had invited Emilie and Tristan to join them for their harvest feast and stay through the weekend. She wanted to introduce Adelina and Emilie, but when she looked for Adelina to ask her, the woman had left.

21

____

Ivy woke at dawn to a pink sunrise through the palm trees. She slipped from beneath the warm duvet, careful not to wake Bennett, who deserved another hour of sleep.

This was the day of their harvest feast, a day of gratitude and shared blessings, of food and laughter, of family and friends.

Thanksgiving.

Her mother's words sprang to mind.

The act of giving thanks for life's blessings.

If only her mother were here, but her parents were so far away. Still, she was happy knowing they were having a wonderful time and still going strong at this stage of their lives. She would call them a little later with her siblings.

This was a quiet moment before people would begin to arrive.

The only guests in residence at the inn were Gilda, Caleb, and a young, high-spirited Italian couple blogging about their travels around the world. The next stops for them were Hawaii and Japan.

Their guests were invited to the feast because all the restaurants were closed, and the aromas from the kitchen would be sheer torture if they weren't included. Today, everyone was family.

She shrugged into her robe, padded across chilly wooden floors, and slid her feet into furry house boots. The day looked cold and clear at the beach, a perfect day for the gathering.

But she didn't have time to linger in their small kitchen with a cup of coffee she desperately needed. She had to dress and continue the preparations for the evening dinner they'd planned for three dozen people.

Including the guests at the inn, she realized the count was more than that. The younger generation often brought friends and dates, too.

Nevertheless, she loved this day with all the faces of people special to them gathered around the tables. Few stayed sour for long when there was so much food and so many different people to talk to.

Even Darla smiled on Thanksgiving.

Ivy dressed quickly in dark corduroy trousers and a warm, emerald-green top that brought out her eyes. She hurried to the main house. She scooped coffee and started it, then mixed and poured batter into a muffin tin to bake. At the sound of a car engine, she looked out to see Mitch and Shelly pull into the car court with Daisy and Vanz.

The back door clicked open. Mitch entered first, carrying a cardboard box, his cheeks flushed from the cool morning air.

"You're here early," she said, pleased to see him.

"I need to get those big boy turkeys prepared. Besides, I couldn't sleep. I was too excited to try adding Diya's new spice blends to my turkey rub."

"Sounds daring."

Mitch set down his box and pulled out small bags of spices. "They'll love it. Nothing too wild, though."

Shelly hustled inside with Daisy on her hip. "Good morning. We have a couple of sleepyheads with us."

The little girl yawned. She was still wearing her one-piece pajamas.

Vanz staggered in behind them carrying a folded playpen for Daisy. He looked sleepy and a little dejected.

Ivy could guess why. "I'm setting up a light breakfast here in the kitchen and in the dining room with muffins, granola, fruit, and yogurt. Who's hungry?"

"Everyone, I'm sure. Especially this one." She tapped Daisy's nose. "I'll set up the family table in here. Where are Poppy and Sunny?"

"Probably sleeping in or getting ready. They knew there wasn't much to do for guests this morning."

Ivy left her sister to it. She prepared the breakfast in the dining room for Caleb and the young Italian couple, who were eager to explore the beach today. Gilda rarely came down for breakfast, preferring to write late and sleep in.

After they all ate, Ivy carried food warmers into the ballroom, positioning electric food warming trays along the antique sideboards and long buffet tables they'd arranged as serving stations. Morning light streamed through tall windows, illuminating the space where their guests would gather this evening.

Laughter spilled from the kitchen. Through the

windows, she saw Bennett take off down the beach for his run.

The household was awake. Ivy loved this time of day before a holiday gathering. The preparations, the laughter, and the inevitable culinary misses that would need to be salvaged.

Minor, she hoped.

Shelly brought in a tray of miniature pumpkins she'd hollowed out to hold candles and small pots of marigolds in the golden colors of the season. "These came out better than I expected."

Positioning the centerpieces on trivets, Shelly placed them on round tables draped with cream-colored tablecloths. She arranged burnt-orange burlap artfully around each centerpiece.

"I love how you wrapped golden twine around the pots," Ivy said, admiring her sister's handiwork. "Where did you leave Daisy?"

"She's being spoiled by Vanz in the kitchen. Daisy makes him laugh, and he treats her like a doll. Until she has a meltdown, of course. Mitch can handle that. It's his turn."

Ivy enjoyed hearing about her sister's approach to motherhood. She also suspected Vanz needed special attention today. She recalled how difficult it had been being away from home on holidays when she lived in Boston.

Ivy reached for a basket. On her morning walks, she had been collecting driftwood for decorating accents, along with shells, which she would return to the beach after the holiday.

Shelly adjusted an arrangement. "The kitchen smells amazing already."

"It's only beginning," Ivy said, adding shells to the centerpiece arrangements. "Wait until Mitch's turkeys go into the oven. He has a strict schedule for every dish."

"I saw that. I'm staying out here where it's safe." Shelly slid copper chargers beneath white plates. Next, she arranged sunflowers in tall, vintage crystal vases she'd found in the old butler's pantry for the buffet table. Satisfied, she paused and turned to Ivy.

"If you haven't noticed, Vanz is a little sad today," Shelly said. "He talked to his mother yesterday, and she promised she would take a bus here, but he hasn't heard from her. None of us have. I've spoken to her on the phone, and I didn't think she was like that. But I've never met her, so I don't know."

"That's a shame, but we'll take care of him today."

Ivy returned to the kitchen to check on the cooking progress.

The room hummed with activity. Mitch rubbed one turkey with garlic and olive oil and basted another one in butter. Every surface had been transformed into a designated workstation with ingredients arranged in order.

Poppy had joined them and was slicing vegetables. Occasionally, she stirred cranberries simmering with orange zest on the stove. Vanz was plowing through the muffins, and Daisy was in her highchair, making a mess with granola and blueberries, but she was happy.

Mitch lifted his chin toward the new electric ovens. "Glad you added those. We couldn't produce this meal with just the original vintage gas oven. These birds are too big to even fit in there."

"Can we use that one for the bread and pies?" Ivy said.

Mitch glanced up. "Check the schedule. Every dish has

its time slot. No jumping the line. The turkeys will cook long and slow."

She glanced at the clock. "Has Sunny been down this morning? I thought she'd be up by now."

Poppy chopped a potato with sudden vigor. "Maybe she's sleeping in."

Ivy frowned. "That's not like her on a holiday. I should check on her. I hope she's not sick."

Just then, Daisy screamed and tried to escape the highchair.

"Oh no, sweetie," Ivy said, hurrying to catch her.

Daisy had eaten the blueberries on her tray, but she wanted the ones that dropped onto the floor.

"Not those, little one." Ivy gave her freshly washed berries, then swept up the rest on the floor.

"I'll check on Sunny," Poppy said.

"Thanks, I appreciate that."

Poppy quickly rinsed and dried her hands before she rushed out.

Caleb wandered into the kitchen. "Mind if I have breakfast in here? The other couple left, and it's lonely in the dining room. It sounds like you're having fun in here. Smells incredible already."

Ivy looked up and smiled. "Sounds like you miss going home."

"It's hard to travel back for such a short holiday."

Ivy placed another basket of spiced pumpkin muffins on the table. "Make yourself comfortable. We're all family today. How is your search for clinic space going?"

"I've found an old house that will work for my veterinary office," he replied. "I can move in before Christmas. I could live in a back room for now, but I'd like to find a different home soon."

"I'm glad for you, even though we'll miss you here." Ivy thought Caleb would be a good addition to Summer Beach. She scrambled the eggs and sprinkled chives on them.

She served Caleb and then glanced at the time. "If you'll excuse me, I should check on Poppy now. I think I've lost both the girls."

Just then, the front door opened, and voices rang out in the foyer. Moments later, Sunny appeared in the kitchen doorway, cheeks flushed from the morning chill. Poppy was beside her, and behind them was a very familiar face.

"Surprise!" Sunny shouted, beaming.

"Happy Thanksgiving, everyone!" Misty stepped forward, a worn backpack slung over one shoulder and her hair pulled into a messy ponytail. She grinned and dropped her backpack.

"Misty?" Ivy gasped. "I thought you couldn't make it." She opened her arms wide with glee.

Misty fell into her mother's arms. "My scenes wrapped early on set, which almost never happens. I called Sunny last night when I confirmed a flight. I wanted to surprise you."

Ivy enveloped her eldest daughter in a tight embrace. She turned to Sunny with tears of joy in her eyes. "I thought you were still sleeping."

Sunny gave her a mischievous smile. "I asked Poppy to cover for me while I shot off to the airport."

"You knew?" Ivy asked, looking at Poppy.

Poppy held up her hands. "I was sworn to secrecy."

Shelly raced in to see Misty, and even Daisy joined in the welcome.

"Perfect timing," Mitch said. "There is plenty to eat."

"Thank goodness, I'm starving. I slept through the breakfast service on the plane." Misty's words died as she caught sight of the guest at the kitchen table.

Her eyebrows shot up. "Caleb?"

The veterinarian had half-risen from his chair, his expression also one of shock. "Misty?"

The kitchen fell silent, tension crystallizing in the air.

Ivy's gaze darted between them. "You two know each other?"

Neither answered immediately.

Finally, Caleb broke the silence. "We met in Los Angeles."

"Before I left for New Zealand," Misty added, a slight tremor in her voice. "Why are you here? Are you stalking me?"

"I would never. You know me better than that."

"Clearly, I don't know anything about you. Why would you visit my family's inn?"

Caleb ran a hand through his hair. "I'm starting a practice here. You told me you were from Boston. You never mentioned Summer Beach."

"Neither did you."

Sunny's eyes widened with realization. "Wait. Is *this* the guy you were talking about?"

"Don't," Misty hissed, a flush creeping up her neck.

Ivy cleared her throat, trying to reduce the tension. "Well, this is unexpected. But it's Thanksgiving, and everyone is hungry. Misty, have a seat, and I'll start your breakfast."

Caleb pulled out a chair for Misty.

She hesitated, then carefully selected a chair that put

maximum distance between herself and Caleb. "Red-eye flights are brutal."

Sunny, Poppy, and Shelly joined them, talking over each other as they peppered Misty with questions about the film and New Zealand.

Conversations resumed as plates were passed and coffee poured. Ivy watched Misty and Caleb studiously avoid eye contact, each speaking only to those seated nearest them. There was a story there she'd probably hear about later.

When Caleb finished his breakfast, he thanked Ivy and excused himself. To Misty, he said in a thick voice, "See you around."

Misty dipped her chin in response and watched him go. Once he was gone, she drew her hands over her face. "Of all the men to find in the kitchen."

"And I thought I was the queen of the awkward moments," Shelly said. "I can't believe you know the hot tattooed veterinarian." She glanced at Mitch. "Sorry, babe. You're hotter, though."

Mitch grinned. "You're only saying that because I feed you."

"You have to admit, that's pretty hot." Shelly laughed. "But really, spill it all, Misty."

Misty shrugged between bites. "I don't know if you'd call it dating. My French press broke, so I went out for coffee one morning and all the tables were taken. I sat next to him at the coffee bar, and we started talking. That went on and on. I still haven't replaced the French press."

"Neither would I," Shelly said. When Mitch threw her a look, she looked sheepish. "Sorry, babe. Figure of speech."

Misty shook her head. "He was like my best friend, but

it was more than that. We just fit. After a couple of days, we'd walk a little after coffee, and a couple of times we met for a cup at the beach. We didn't see each other for very long, but it was magical. We talked about everything and nothing at all."

"Everything but Summer Beach," Sunny said.

Misty shook her head. "I knew Caleb wanted out of L.A. And he should have known how much I wanted that part in the film. We were in a bubble of our own making, I guess. Then, the original actor fell ill. My agent called and asked how fast I could get myself to Auckland. I didn't have a chance to say goodbye to Caleb. I missed our morning brew and didn't call him until I landed, and it was a long flight. He said he was worried about me and disappointed. And that was the last time we ever talked."

"Is that what you wanted?" Ivy asked.

"No, but I needed that part."

Ivy understood. They each had their goals, and they hadn't been honest with each other. Clearly, they would have some emotional currents to navigate today.

Caleb came downstairs with a small bag. "I think it's best that I find another place through the holidays."

Panic flashed across Misty's face. "You don't mean that, do you?"

"I'm not going to interfere with you and your family on a holiday weekend."

"Let's go for a walk first," Misty said, rising.

He shook his head, but Misty had already put on her jacket and opened the back door. With a heavy sigh, he relented, setting down his bag to follow her.

They all watched them go.

"Wow," Shelly said, her eyes round. "That was like a

scene from a movie. Misty's a boss, and I didn't even realize it."

Laughter bubbled around the kitchen.

Ivy poured another cup of coffee and watched them walk toward the shoreline. "She's grown up."

"I wonder what they're talking about," Poppy said.

Behind them, Mitch opened an oven door and slid in a turkey. He repeated that two more times, putting each turkey in its place.

"Bravo," Shelly said.

"Pies are up now," Poppy said, rising to confirm the scheduled time. She put the one she'd finished this morning into the vintage oven where the muffins had baked. "I'll cycle the pies through, so we'll have plenty."

Mitch set the timer. "The turkeys will come out just before dinner. I'll start some other dishes, but first, a break."

He joined them at the table, tickling Daisy until she laughed.

Suddenly, a sharp crack rang somewhere outside, followed by a deep, ominous boom. The overhead lights flickered once, twice, and then died. The refrigerators powered down with a dimming hum, and the digital clock on the new oven blinked out.

In the sudden silence, the only sounds were the old oven's gas flame and the tick of a battery-operated clock on the wall.

Mitch pushed back his chair. "That didn't sound good."

"Must be a power outage," Shelly said. "I wonder if it's just us."

Mitch strode to the oven and yanked open the door. Heat still radiated from within, but the heating elements no longer glowed. "The turkeys are just getting started," he reported grimly. "I'll check the breakers in the service room."

While he was gone, Shelly peered outside. "I don't see lights anywhere else."

"Maybe it's just a glitch," Ivy said. "I'm sure the electricity will come back on soon."

Mitch returned, shaking his head.

"I'll call the electric company," Shelly said. However, all she got was a busy signal. "Their lines must be jammed with calls."

They waited as the minutes stretched on, but nothing changed. The kitchen remained dim, illuminated only by daylight through the windows.

Bennett jogged inside from the beach and pulled out his phone. "Did you see that? Looked like a transformer malfunction. I'll call emergency services."

Ivy watched as he spoke in low tones, her optimism fading with every frown. When he hung up, his expression confirmed her fears.

"A power grid issue caused that, so the problem is more widespread than thought." He hesitated. "They're calling in a team."

"How long will the power be out?" Mitch asked.

Bennett rubbed his chin. "They're not sure, but probably a few hours."

Shelly took Mitch's hand. "I'm sorry about your turkeys, babe."

"It's not just ours," he said. "Most everyone in town is cooking a turkey right now. Unless they have gas ovens, they're all in trouble."

Ivy looked around the large kitchen. "We can cook one

turkey in the old oven, but that won't be enough for everyone. What about Java Beach?"

Mitch shook his head. "Electric ovens, gas cooktop. Not good for cooking a turkey whole. What's the alternative?"

"Forrest and Flint. Maybe we can cook there." Shelly tapped their numbers.

Chaos ensued as everyone began talking at once, suggestions overlapping into a rise of increasingly desperate ideas.

After speaking with their brothers, Shelly shook her head. "They're also without power, and they have electric ovens and cooktops. They're on their way over, and we'll figure out something. This might be the feast of cold salads."

"Not without refrigeration," Mitch said. "Keep the doors shut, or we'll lose everything if the power doesn't come back on in a few hours."

Everyone grumbled at that.

Misty and Caleb came into the kitchen. "We heard the noise. What happened?"

"An equipment malfunction in Arizona took down the grid from there into Southern California and down to Mexico," Bennett replied. "That blew out a local transformer. The grid and equipment will take a while to repair, so the city is issuing an emergency alert. The hospital has a backup generator, and we're recommending people go there if they have medical devices or health needs. The shelter also has a generator for power, so that's another place people can go for food and warmth."

Ivy was glad to hear that. She thought about Adelina and the others she'd met at the shelter. Now she wished she'd invited the older woman, but perhaps she had made friends there. Still, they'd had a connection, and she wanted to get to know her better and try to help her if she could. Guilt twisted in her chest.

"This sounds serious." Mitch pushed a hand through his hair. "Even if the electricity comes on within three hours, dinner will be late. Any more than that, and we'll be eating at midnight."

"And if it's later?" Ivy asked.

Mitch raised his hands. "We'll get very creative."

Everyone groaned, but Shelly stood and raised her hands. "How about some Sea Breeze cocktails while we wait? I'm willing to sacrifice some ice cubes."

22

Ivy stood in the kitchen, staring at the cold oven as if willpower alone might resurrect it with a jolt of electricity. Bennett's latest conversation with the electric company had confirmed her worst fears. There would be no power until much later.

Their fabulous harvest feast was rapidly unraveling.

"We'll figure out something," Bennett said, sliding his phone into his pocket. "We always do." He kissed her cheek. "I'll take a quick shower and be right back."

Ivy watched him go, and as she did, she saw a strange car pull into the car court.

She stepped outside to see a woman with auburn hair emerge from the back of a dusty car. The woman held her arms out to Vanz.

The teenager raced toward her. "Mom, you made it."

His mother wrapped her arms tightly around her son. "I couldn't miss this day with you, honey. I love you so much, and I'm sorry for all you've had to endure."

Tears sprang to the boy's eyes. "I wish I could have protected you."

"That wasn't your job," she whispered. "But things will be better now."

Vanz blinked back tears and turned to introduce everyone. "I guess you figured out this is my mom."

Mitch stepped forward. "It's good to see you again, Melinda."

"You were awfully young," she said, hugging him. "We all were. Thank you for taking him in while I worked out that mess. It means a lot to me. To us. I hope we're not imposing too much."

"Not at all," Shelly said, embracing her. "You're welcome to stay with us, too."

Vanz hovered near his mother, looking more protective than Ivy had ever seen him.

Ivy saw fatigue etched into Melinda's face, and her eyes mirrored her son's. Their eyes were kind but haunted, as if they'd seen too much. "We're happy to have you. Unfortunately, we're without electricity now. It's not too cold, and we have fireplaces throughout. We might be cooking in them later."

She invited Melinda inside to relax and have a bite to eat in the kitchen while they continued with food preparations, despite the uncertainty about the electricity.

"I understand you're thinking about relocating to Summer Beach," Shelly said to Melinda as they walked through the rear door.

The other woman nodded. "Vanz is happier than he has been in years. I'd like to find work right away so we can have a small place of our own."

While they were working in the kitchen, Bennett

returned. As he walked in, his phone buzzed. He stepped away to answer it, his expression growing more concerned with each passing second.

"Looks like the electricity will be off all day and maybe until morning," he announced when he returned. "The damage to the electrical grid is more extensive than previously thought. It's a wide-scale outage."

Sunny appeared in the doorway, wrapped in an orange sweater. "Is Thanksgiving canceled?"

"Not canceled, just reimagined." As Ivy spoke, an idea occurred to her. "We can fire up the grills on the patio. Let's talk to Mitch."

When everyone gathered in the kitchen, Bennett filled them in. A chorus of disappointment swept across the room.

"It's not as bad as it sounds," Ivy said, looking for hope in the situation. "Mitch, we can cook on the outdoor gas grills, can't we?"

Mitch brightened at the idea. "The large grill has hoods. I can probably roast the turkeys and anything that needs to be covered and baked. We can use the open grill for everything else. Then there's the grill at Java Beach. We could butterfly the turkeys or cut them up and cook by lantern light if needed. So yeah, we can make this work. No one will starve tonight."

Bennett stroked his chin. "Great ideas. There must be a lot of families with half-cooked turkeys. Some may not have gas stoves or outdoor grills."

"I could get mine from the house," Mitch said. "We can fire it up on the patio, and anyone who wants to come by can use it."

Ivy liked the idea. "We have plenty of seating inside or

on the patio under heat lamps. Everyone is welcome to bring what they have and cook here."

Poppy spoke up. "I can ask Dad to bring his grill when he comes. He has one he uses for football tailgate parties. Uncle Flint, too."

Bennett put his arm around Ivy. "Shall we spread the word and make it a community barbecue on the beach?"

She grinned. "You bet. Let's save Thanksgiving."

Poppy pitched in. "We can call people and check on them. They can bring their food, and we'll finish cooking it together."

"I'll call my staff and see how they're doing," Mitch said. "They can open Java Beach if they want."

Vanz's mother raised her hand. "I can pitch in. I worked in a restaurant."

Mitch shook his head. "You're family. You're with us, and I'll spread the word for you. I know a couple of places that might be hiring."

"The weather isn't that cold," Ivy said. "I don't think our new gas heater will come on without electricity, but we have plenty of duvets we can use tonight. And fireplaces. They're all original." She'd planned to light the large fireplace in the grand ballroom tonight.

They talked about lanterns and candles, and Bennett put people in charge of those. He grinned. "We have a plan. Let's all go to work."

While everyone scattered, Bennett caught Ivy's hand. "Sweetheart, has anyone heard from Emilie and Tristan? I'm concerned about them making the drive with the streetlights out."

"They're used to living in the country where it's dark," Ivy said. "But I worry about the other drivers who aren't. I tried to reach Emilie on Shelly's phone, but my calls go to voicemail. They might be in an area where the calls drop."

Bennett furrowed his brow. "If they decide to come, I hope they're okay."

"They might have stayed at the vineyard, given the power outage. But I'll let you know if I hear from them."

While others checked the rooms to make sure each one had flashlights and lanterns, Ivy helped Mitch in the kitchen.

She was at the counter preparing miniature potato stacks with rosemary from the garden when she saw her nephew Reed's large work vehicle pull into the car court. She called out to Poppy, "Your brother is here. Maybe he brought a grill with him."

Poppy hurried outside. Suddenly, she screamed.

"What's going on?" Ivy dried her hands and followed her.

When the doors to the vehicle opened, Ivy caught her breath as her parents emerged.

"Grandma!" Poppy raced to greet Carlotta.

In an instant, Ivy was right beside her, hugging her mother as well.

Sterling wrapped his arms around Ivy. "How's my lovely middle daughter?"

"Dad, I can't believe you're here." She tightened her arms around him, then her mother joined in the group hug. "What an amazing surprise. I thought you were in South Africa."

Carlotta's sun-kissed face lit up. "Surprise, darling! We were, but after seeing Honey and Gabe in Sydney—they send their love, by the way—we realized spending the holiday away from the rest of our children just didn't seem right. As much fun as we've been having sailing the high seas, we were homesick for all of you. So we decided to take our break here."

Grinning, Sterling rubbed his shoulder. "It turns out we need more rest between ports. So we thought, why not take turns hanging out with our kids through the new year? If you'll have us, that is."

"We'd all love that," Ivy said, squeezing her arms around them. "I have a room for you right now. Do you have your luggage?"

"Sure do," her father replied. "Reed picked us up from the airport."

Carlotta's silver bangles jingled as she raised her hands to her cheeks in surprise. "My goodness, is that Misty?"

Misty flew from the house to greet her grandparents, with Sunny right behind her. Caleb stood at the door, watching the scene with a smile.

"I'll tell everyone you're here," Ivy said, leaving her parents. She paused next to Caleb. "This has certainly turned into an unusual day for you, hasn't it?"

Caleb chuckled. "I hope you don't think I was creeping around here to get close to Misty. I had no idea she was part of your family, or even from Summer Beach."

"Technically, she's never lived here. She wasn't lying when she told you she's from Boston. That's where my daughters grew up. Misty moved out before I came here, and then she settled in Los Angeles."

He cast a look of amazement toward Misty. "I keep asking myself, what were the chances we'd run into each other here? This blows my mind."

"Have you worked out your differences now?"

Caleb nodded thoughtfully. "We had a very good talk on the beach. It was well overdue."

A sense of *déjà vu* coursed through Ivy, as if she'd had this conversation before. She knew she hadn't, but had something like this transpired before right here on this spot?

With the history of this house, that was entirely possible. How many people had fallen in love here? At that thought, a warm sense of nostalgia filled her.

Ivy was glad they'd had a chance to get to know Caleb before Misty arrived. She had witnessed his gentleness in caring for animals and heard Emilie speak highly of him. But what mattered more was that he and Misty seemed to have fallen for each other.

Ivy placed a hand on Caleb's shoulder. "I've learned this old house brings people together in the most unusual ways."

Maybe Misty and Caleb's feelings would turn to love, but it was too soon to tell. Misty still had a dream to pursue; they both did. She wouldn't push her daughters, yet she would welcome those they cared about, just as her parents had.

Someday, her family might expand. That possibility still seemed far away, but it could happen anytime.

Carlotta appeared behind her and hooked her arm through Ivy's. "It's wonderful to see you. We decided family matters more than adventure. Now, where's your sister and that little Daisy? I imagine she's grown since I saw her last."

"Not only is she walking now, but she's running. We can hardly keep up with her, and she's parroting everything we say. Let's go find them."

As they wove through dim hallways, Ivy explained the situation with the electrical outage and the cooking challenges. "We'll have lanterns out shortly. And dinner by candlelight."

"As long as we can see everyone, that's all that matters. We can eat cold beans and tortillas for all I care."

"You won't have to. Mitch is firing up the grills."

As they walked through the bustling activity at the inn, Carlotta surprised and hugged everyone in turn.

Ivy's heart filled with love and appreciation as everything she'd hoped for had come to pass. Misty and her parents were here. Against all odds, most of her family was together again, except for her oldest sister. Honey and Gabe often visited their daughter, Elena, in Los Angeles, so Ivy hoped they could also reunite soon.

She drew a breath, wondering how many more twists and surprises this day might hold. She realized she could stress over the sudden change of plans the power outage had brought, or she could enjoy these rare moments of surprise.

She peeked into a room where Shelly was replacing batteries in flashlights. Her sister's reaction to seeing their mother was instant, and her face lit with joy.

"Mom!" Shelly cried, flinging herself into Carlotta's arms. "Oh, my gosh, I can't believe you're here. This day just went from tragic to fantastic. Is Dad with you?"

"Of course, he's somewhere behind me." Carlotta framed Shelly's face with her hands. "*Mija*, my darling. And your precious Daisy. I want to hear everything."

Ivy left them to catch up while she prepared for more guests.

A little later, Forrest and Flint arrived with their families. Their adult children, most in their twenties, were excited about the unexpected barbecue. Darla came over with her friend Louise, and neighbors began appearing bearing dishes in various stages of completion.

Imani and Clark arrived, as did Jen and George with Jen's sister and her children. Another neighbor brought a portable generator to power a refrigerator.

Bennett's sister and her family came. Even Carol Reston and her husband Hal joined them, saying they'd heard this is where the fun was.

And everyone pitched in to help.

Bennett checked in with Ivy. "Caleb volunteered to help set up the propane heaters on the patio. It's hardly been cold enough to use them yet, but I expect it will be tonight." He paused. "I liked him even before I knew about him and Misty. This is turning out to be a Thanksgiving to remember."

"On so many levels." She kissed him before they went their separate ways. Even though the scene was chaotic, her heart was so full of love for everyone she encountered.

On the expansive rear patio, Bennett and Caleb positioned propane heaters in strategic locations around the pool, creating pockets of warmth around which people could gather. They stacked firewood near the fire pit on the sand, preparing for the evening chill that would descend after sunset.

Sunny and Misty unfurled extra tablecloths over more tables inside, while Poppy put out cutlery. Outside, they decided to use thick paper plates and plastic glasses for poolside dining.

Ivy moved through the increasingly crowded inn, answering questions and enjoying the holiday vibe. The disaster had transformed the planned family gathering into an unexpected extravaganza that included old and new friends, far beyond anything she might have planned.

"We need more serving utensils and platters," she told Poppy, who was organizing the buffet stations. "Check the upper cabinets in the butler's pantry."

A neighbor recharged her phone with his generator, and now her phone buzzed with messages from friends responding to her calls. Many were on their way and spreading the word.

"There's a party at the inn," she heard someone say on their phone. "Bring your hibachi. Everyone is cooking out on the beach, and they have the fire pit going. Bring your guitar."

They'd soon have music on the beach. She smiled to herself, expecting that Bennett would join in with his guitar. This was how they celebrated in Summer Beach.

Ivy paused in the doorway of the kitchen, watching Mitch demonstrate turkey carving techniques to several people. Misty was helping Sunny arrange desserts on the buffet while Caleb was unpacking more lanterns.

Children's laughter rang out as they played impromptu games of tag between the tables. Shelly had set up a kids' area with blankets to build forts and card games for the older kids. Vanz sat nearby with Daisy on his lap, reading to her while Melinda, already looking more relaxed, helped arrange silverware.

Ivy's phone buzzed, and she answered. It was Emilie, saying they had just passed through the mountains and Summer Beach was in sight.

Emilie sounded mesmerized. "We're enjoying a beautiful drive. The night is clear, and the stars are coming out over the ocean. We'll see you soon."

Ivy chatted with her and then hung up.

Bennett stopped beside her. "Was that Emilie?"

"They're on their way. Not too far away now."

"That's a relief," Bennett said. "It's great seeing everyone here, isn't it?"

An idea occurred to her. "Not quite everyone. I need to go to the shelter. It won't take long. Remember the woman I told you about?"

Bennett kissed her forehead. "Let's get our jackets."

The harvest feast activities were taking on a life of their own, with Mitch directing the culinary endeavors. Poppy and Sunny were acting as hosts, while Shelly tended to the children.

"Quick, before anyone stops us," Ivy said.

They slipped out the back door and took his vehicle.

Ivy clicked her seat belt and shoulder strap. "I don't know if Adelina is still at the shelter, but with her connection to our house through her father, I have a strong feeling that she should be with us. I don't think she has anyone else, and she's grieving the loss of her husband."

Bennett reached for her hand and kissed it. "We both know how that feels, don't we? Your heart is in the right place."

"I hope she's not insulted that I didn't invite her sooner. I wish I'd thought of it, but I knew the shelter was planning a feast."

"You had a lot on your mind."

In a few minutes, they arrived. Bennett parked in front of the shelter. Inside at the desk, they asked for Adelina.

"I don't think she's with us anymore," the younger woman behind the counter said.

Ivy's heart sank. "Do you know where she might have

gone?"

"I'm sorry, no." The volunteer shook her head and returned to her work.

They were just about to leave when Ivy glanced through an open door. She saw the other woman, sitting alone. "She's here," she cried.

The younger woman looked up. "Oh, you mean Addie. I'll get her."

When Adelina emerged, she looked pleasantly surprised. "I thought you'd be with your family."

Ivy quickly explained. "Would you like to come to the inn for our harvest feast? It's a little chaotic, but it's turning out to be a lot of fun. And I would love for you to meet our friends. We also have an open guest room and would love to have you for the weekend."

Bennett interjected, "I have to warn you, we have no power, but we have lanterns, candles, barbecue, and fireplaces."

"It's quite cozy," Ivy added.

"What a generous offer," Adelina said, happiness blooming on her face. "I appreciate your thinking of me, but this is rather sudden."

Ivy touched her arm. "Art is often about the unexpected, isn't it?"

The silver-haired woman smiled at that. "It won't take me long to gather my things."

After Adelina left, Bennett turned to Ivy. "This is one more reason why I love you."

"I feel like she belongs with us this weekend. I want to show her the logs from the bunker and the photos we took. If her father kept those logs, they'll have special meaning to her. Imagine if she recognizes his handwriting."

"You're a wonder." He kissed her on the cheek.

Adelina returned with a small bag, and Bennett carried it for her. He helped her into his vehicle, and soon they were on their way.

When they arrived at the inn, the rooms were lit with lanterns and the glow of the fireplaces. Inside, Ivy introduced Adelina to her parents, thinking they might have things in common to talk about.

"My parents have just arrived," Ivy said, leading her to where Carlotta and Sterling were seated by the fire.

Carlotta stood with an expression of surprise on her face. "Why, Adelina, how nice to see you. Sterling, you remember Adelina. We represented her glasswork and mosaics to some of the finest stores."

Ivy was pleased they knew each other. Her parents were well known among artists for placing original arts and crafts with high-end department stores and galleries before they retired.

"You'll have plenty of time to catch up," Ivy said. "Adelina will be staying with us for a few days." And in that time, she hoped they could figure out a way for the older woman to revive her career and leave the shelter.

Emilie and Tristan arrived shortly afterward with a wine bag, a selection of cheeses, and winter vegetables from their garden.

"This is part of our harvest," Emilie said, handing Ivy a lovely gift bag.

"And how was the drive?" Bennett asked.

"Without glaring lights, except for other cars, everything is soft on the eyes," Tristan said as he opened the wine and poured glasses for them and Ivy's parents. "It reminds me of being in the country in France."

Sunny came by with appetizers from the grill, offering stuffed mushrooms, zucchini, and shrimp on skewers.

People were sharing what they'd brought, and Ivy loved that. The food coming off the grills smelled delicious.

She introduced Emilie and Tristan to Adelina, and soon they were all talking about art glass. As Emilie described her blown glass chandelier of grapes and leaves, a smile grew on Adelina's face. She brought out her phone and scrolled to her portfolio.

"This one?" The image shone against the flickering firelight.

"Why, that's it," Emilie exclaimed, moving closer.

"I was quite proud of that one," Adelina said, sharing her work.

A little later, when Ivy showed Adelina a beautiful vintage piece in the fancy powder room off the ballroom, the woman's face brightened again.

"That is one of my father's pieces. He told me he designed items for the Ericksons' home. He referred to it as Las Brisas del Mar."

"And what are you doing now?" Carol Reston asked with keen interest.

"Not as much as I would like. It's been a tumultuous period in my life." Adelina told them her story and about her husband's recent demise.

Ivy could tell she was a little embarrassed by her circumstances.

Nevertheless, Adelina shared her situation, adding, "I hope to restart my career. I had a good feeling about Summer Beach, and the shelter had space available for me."

Bennett put his arm around Ivy. "When you said you

thought Adelina should be here, I wasn't sure what you meant."

"Neither was I. But look at how she's come to life. I think she's brave for sharing her story."

"She might have some new clients, too."

A thought occurred to Ivy. "I just heard about a new artist project with shared workspaces here in town. I don't know much about it, but I'll check on that for her."

"I hope you don't mind, but I told Carol and Hal about the bunker," Bennett said. "They're fascinated by it, and your idea of making it part of the library and art museum complex."

Ivy was relieved to hear that. Maybe they could raise private funds to preserve the bunker. "Don't forget the public art I mentioned. And Shelly's instructional garden."

"I'm listening to you from now on," Bennett said. "They expressed interest in seeing the bunker and helping to maintain it. Hal's father served in the military, so he has a keen interest. I showed him the log."

"You brought it up from the bunker?"

Bennett looked sheepish. "I was trying to make out some of the notes. I've been careful with it."

She watched the group talking and enjoying themselves. "They're having such a good time. Let's share the log with Adelina when we have better light."

In her heart, Ivy already knew there would be a connection, and another piece of the past would emerge through the veil of history. The researchers and historians would also return to inspect the space and share what they'd found.

She could see it all unfolding in her mind. But those events were for another day.

Now, she simply wanted to be in the moment, enjoying the family and friends who meant so much to her.

Mitch came inside and clapped his hands. "The turkeys are ready, so dinner is served. It's a Seabreeze Inn harvest feast. Come eat, folks."

While everyone got up to go to the buffet, Bennett took Ivy's hand. "Just a moment. Let's go look at the stars on the beach while they line up."

"I could use a little break," Ivy said, squeezing his hand. It had been such a busy, nonstop day.

They strolled outside onto the beach. The fire pit was glowing with flames crackling against the sound of the ocean waves. They lingered by the fire, enjoying the warmth. Overhead, stars blanketed the sky with a blaze of starlight, like pinpricks of light in a velvet sky that fell to the sea.

Without lights from roads and communities illuminating the coastline, the effect was magical. She'd never seen it like this.

"Thanks for bringing me out here," she said, kissing him softly.

"We have a lot to be grateful for." Bennett brought his arms around her. "Happy Thanksgiving, sweetheart."

She gazed at him, his face glowing in the firelight. "It's even happier than I imagined. Who knew that a major inconvenience could turn out to be something to be thankful for? This is a day we'll never forget."

"A magical day like no other," he said, tightening his embrace when she shivered.

"It certainly is." The warmth of his skin was comforting and inviting. "I think almost every day holds a little magic —if we take the time to realize it."

He gazed at her with curiosity. "In what way?"

"Think about the coincidences, hunches, premonitions, and surprise courtesies we usually take for granted. And above all, love."

"Interesting insights," he said, nodding thoughtfully.

"Like today," she mused. "A beautiful experience was created from unexpected circumstances. A power outage threatened to ruin our celebration. Instead, it stripped away barriers and brought people together."

Bennett's breath warmed her neck, and he looked into her eyes. "I have a good feeling about everyone gathered here. And a wonderful feeling about us."

Laughter bubbled up in her throat, and she threw her head back. "If you're just realizing that, my dear husband, you're a little late."

His eyes twinkled in the firelight. "Not if you believe the best is yet to come."

"It is, isn't it? Even when it's unplanned." She believed every day brought new opportunities and deepened her love for her husband.

"That's the real magic," he said, nuzzling her cheek. "Letting life unfold and accepting the challenges, however great they may be. That's what I love about you."

She leaned into his embrace, letting his words wash over her, blanketing her with the warmth of his love.

Together, they watched their family and friends gather around the barbecue. Here were people who, like them, had chosen to transform challenge into celebration. Once again, the inn was a home and haven for more than just those who lived within its walls.

Ivy sighed happily. "These are our people, and I love every one of them."

Bennett pulled back slightly and arched a brow, teasing her. "What about me?"

Ivy laughed softly. "I will love you as long as those waves kiss this beach. I'm so thankful for us."

She touched her lips to his with all the gratitude in her heart.

THANK you for reading *Seabreeze Harvest*, and I hope you enjoyed the harvest feast at the Seabreeze Inn. Download a free extra bonus read:

JanMoran.com/SeabreezeHarvestBonusScene

NEXT: Read *Seabreeze Garden*. Everyone is welcoming spring, but the season brings more surprises and challenges at the inn.

BONUS! Discover more in Summer Beach. Download your free Summer Beach Welcome Kit now!

JanMoran.com/SummerBeachWelcomeKit

SHOP: Keep up with my new releases on my website and online shop at JanMoran.com. You can shop exclusive ebook, paperback, and audiobook bundles ONLY on my bookshop at store.JanMoran.com.

JOIN: Please join my VIP Reader's Club to receive news about special deals and new releases. Plus, find more fun and join other like-minded readers in my Facebook Reader's Group.

MORE: Want more beach fun? Check out my popular Coral Cottage and Crown Island series and meet the boisterous, fun-loving Moore-Delavie and Raines families, who are always up to something.

Looking for sunshine and international travel? Meet a group of friends in a series all about sunshine, style, and second chances, beginning with Flawless and an exciting trip to Paris.

Finally, I invite you to read my immersive family sagas, including *Hepburn's Necklace* and *The Chocolatier*, 1950s novels set in gorgeous Italy.

Most of my books are available in ebook, paperback, hardcover, audiobook, and large print. And as always, I wish you happy reading!

SEABREEZE HARVEST RECIPES

Potato Stacks with Herbs & Garlic

These are the potato stacks that Ivy prepared for the harvest feast dinner. You'll enjoy this layered stack of crispy, thinly sliced potatoes made in muffin tins. These may be made with butter and Parmesan cheese or dairy-free with olive oil. Both are delicious.

Yellow or red-skinned potatoes work best, such as German Butterball or Yukon Gold. These smaller, less starchy potatoes are about the diameter of a muffin tin. The resulting tower will be crispy on the outside and soft on the inside.

For variations on the theme, try different herbs, such as rosemary, oregano, thyme, parsley, or a combination of your favorites. These can be made ahead; simply refrigerate them in the muffin tin and finish before serving.

Ingredients:

Herb Butter or Olive Oil Mixture

½ cup (100 g) unsalted butter or olive oil, or a blend
3 garlic cloves, minced, or to taste
3 Tbsp chopped fresh rosemary (plus small sprigs for garnish)
1 tsp kosher salt, or to taste
Freshly ground black pepper to taste

Potato Stacks

3 lb (1.5 kg) yellow or red potatoes, unpeeled
12 small rosemary sprigs or herb of choice
Optional: ½ cup (50 g) finely grated Parmesan cheese

Instructions:

1. **Preheat the oven** to 375°F (190°C). Lightly grease a 12-cup muffin tin with oil.

2. **Make the herb mixture:** Melt the butter (or warm the oil), then stir in the garlic, chopped rosemary or other herbs, salt, and pepper. Let cool slightly.

3. **Prepare the potatoes:** Using a mandoline or sharp knife, slice the potatoes into very thin rounds (about 1/16 inch).

4. **Combine:** Place the potato slices in a large bowl. Pour the herb mixture over them and toss gently to coat.

5. **Assemble:** Place a small rosemary sprig in the bottom of each muffin cup. Layer the potato slices loosely, allowing edges to overlap. If using Parmesan, sprinkle some midway through stacking, then continue layering. Slightly overfilling is fine. The stacks will compress as they bake.

6. **Bake covered:** Cover the muffin tin tightly with foil and bake for 25 minutes, or until the potatoes are mostly tender.

7. **Bake uncovered:** Remove the foil, increase the oven temperature to 425°F (220°C), and bake for an additional 13–15 minutes, or until the tops and edges are golden and crisp.

8. **Serve:** Let cool for a few minutes. Remove each stack with a fork or small spatula. Flip so the herb sprig on the bottom is upright. Bottom will be crunchy and darker. Sprinkle lightly with kosher salt and serve warm.

Make-Ahead

Bake as directed, then let cool slightly and transfer to a wire rack. Reheat at 350°F (175°C) for approximately 10 minutes, or until thoroughly heated. For extra-crispy edges, finish under the broiler briefly, watching closely.

Spiced Apple Cider

Warm spiced apple cider is a wintry favorite at the Seabreeze Inn. In *Seabreeze Harvest*, Ivy and her family indulge in a cup of hot apple cider in the small town of Julian. This is a real mountain village in Southern California, and I enjoy visiting Julian for some of the best apple cider and apple pie around.

This recipe uses nonalcoholic apple cider, also known as unfiltered, unsweetened apple juice. In some countries, apple cider is an alcoholic beverage.

This recipe is also known as mulled apple cider. Traditional mulling spices for apple cider (or warm mulled wine) are cinnamon, cloves, allspice, nutmeg, and star anise, along with sliced oranges, apples, and lemons.

When the air turns crisp, it's time to enjoy warm apple cider. A side benefit is the lovely aroma that will fill your home.

Makes: About 8 cups (2 L)

Ingredients:

8 cups (2 L) apple cider (nonalcoholic), preferably unfiltered
3 cinnamon sticks
1 tsp (3 g) whole cloves
1 tsp (3 g) whole allspice berries
1 orange, sliced
1/4 cup (50 g) brown sugar (optional, to taste)
1/2 Tbsp (15 mL) vanilla extract (optional)
8 cinnamon sticks for garnish (optional)
orange slices to garnish (optional)

Directions:

1. Combine the ingredients. Pour apple cider into a medium-sized pot. Add cinnamon sticks, cloves, allspice, vanilla, and orange slices. If desired, stir in brown sugar. May also use brown sugar substitutes, such as Splenda brand.

2. Warm. Heat over medium until cider begins to steam. Reduce heat to low.

3. Simmer. Let cider simmer for about 30 minutes to allow flavors to infuse.

4. Strain & serve. Remove the spices and orange slices with strainer. Ladle into mugs. Garnish with cinnamon sticks and orange slices if desired. Optional: A splash of dark rum.

ABOUT THE AUTHOR

JAN MORAN is a *USA Today* and a *Wall Street Journal* bestselling author of romantic women's fiction. A few of her favorite things include a fine cup of coffee, dark chocolate, fresh flowers, laughter, and music that touches her soul. She loves to travel, and her favorite places for inspiration are those rich with history and mystery and set against snowy mountains, palm-treed beaches, or sparkly city lights. Jan is originally from Austin, Texas, and a trace of a drawl still survives, although she has lived in Southern California near the beach for years.

Her books are also available as audiobooks, and many have been translated into other languages, If you enjoyed this book, please consider leaving a brief review online for your fellow readers where you purchased this book or on Goodreads or Bookbub.

To read Jan's other historical and contemporary novels, visit JanMoran.com. Join her VIP Readers Club mailing list and her Facebook Readers Group to learn of new releases, sales, and contests.